I'M MOVING BACK TO MARS
THE OFFICIAL BOOK OF NONSENSE

Fred Wooldridge

1663 Liberty Drive, Suite 200
Bloomington, Indiana 47403
(800) 839-8640
www.AuthorHouse.com

© 2005 Fred Wooldridge. All Rights Reserved.

No part of this book may be reproduced, stored in a retrieval system, or transmitted by any means without the written permission of the author.

First published by AuthorHouse 12/12/05

ISBN: 1-4208-8697-5 (sc)

Library of Congress Control Number: 2005908527

Printed in the United States of America
Bloomington, Indiana

This book is printed on acid-free paper.

Acknowledgments

*Without the support and love of the "little missus"
none of this would have been possible. Maddy has been
at my side from the beginning. I love you.*

*I wish to give a huge thank you to Kim Lewicki,
Publisher/Editor of the Highlands Newspaper for all
her kindness and support. Without her, my writing
juices might have just evaporated.*

*And last, but most importantly, a thank you to all
my readers who religiously read my column. Your
encouragement has made this happen.*

-CONTENTS-

ACKNOWLEDGMENTS   V

CHAPTER ONE
UTTER NONSENSE

I LONG FOR THE GOOD OLD DAYS	*1*
RANDOM THOUGHTS	*4*
FOR WOMEN ONLY	*6*
YIKES, I LOOK LIKE MY FATHER	*9*
I'M OUT OF THE CLOSET!!	*11*
SHE CARRIED A BIG STICKAND NEVER WALKED SOFTLY	*13*
SEX	*16*
CART WARS	*18*
HOW I AVOID TERRORISTS	*21*
NEVER TRUST A MAN WHO........	*24*
BYE BABY BUNTING FRED'S GONE A HUNTING	*26*
TRAFFIC ENFORCEMENT IS DIFFERENT	*29*
SQUIRREL LOVERS, TAKE A PROZAC	*31*
I'M HOPPING MAD AT HOMOSEXUALS	*34*
IS BEING DEAD LIKE HOLDING YOUR BREATH FOREVER?	*37*
FRED'S THEORY OF EVOLUTION	*39*
VOO-DOO BRIDGE	*42*
BEWARE OF CON MEN LIKE ME!	*44*
DON'T BE SHOCKED, MY MENU HAS CHANGED	*46*
SHE IS THE CZAR OF ONE WORD SENTENCES	*49*
DON'T MESS WITH MY THREE LEGGED TREE RAT	*52*
F.W., PHONE HOME	*55*

LADIES, DO NOT READ THIS COLUMN	57
HIGHLANDS NEEDS A FEW GALLUS DOMESTICUS CANNONS	60
NEVER SAY "HMMM"	62
THE RITE OF MAKING MY WRONG RIGHT	65
WHEN I GROW UP, I'M GOING TO BE A FLAG MAN	68
I LOVE DEER HUNTERS	70
I'M DECOMPOSING	73
THE DANGLING CHAD	75
"I'LL SHOW YOU MINE, THEN YOU SHOW ME YOURS"	78
MEET MISTER GRUMP	81
ALL MY REAL ENEMIES ARE FINALLY DEAD	84
WHY GOD INVENTED DEATH	87
VALENTINE'S DAY BAH, HUMBUG	90
STRANGE PLACES I HAVE STUCK MY TONGUE	92
"LET'S TALK TRASH"	95
I AM NOT MAKING THIS UP	97
KITTY HAWK, THE SLUT	99

CHAPTER TWO
DEAR FRED

DEAR POOP	103
DEAR SPACE CADET	104
DEAR NONE OF YOUR BUSINESS (BLUSH)	106
DEAR S.N.O.T.T.	107
DEAR TISH	109
DEAR MP	110
DEAR F.O.O.L.	113
DEAR D.O.A.	114
DEAR SMIT	116
DEAR MS	118

DEAR ANGRY	*119*
DEAR DUH	*121*
HELLO JANICE	*121*

CHAPTER THREE
CHILDREN'S STORIES

MANUEL CARLOS RODRIGUEZ MENDEZ-MACEDO AND THE THREE BEARS	*125*
THE STORY OF WHINNY, THE POOP	*128*
PETER SPAM IN NEVERLAND	*131*
BIG RED RIDING LEAVES THE HOOD	*134*

CHAPTER FOUR
SERIOUS STUFF

SHE HAUNTS MY MEMORY	*137*
PRAISE THE LORD AND PASS THE A BOMBS	*139*
SHE WAS NO "MOTHER TERESA"	*142*
A WALK ON THE MOON	*145*
THE KILLING MACHINE	*148*
FREDDIE, THE LEAF	*151*
INSURANCED OUT	*154*
ONCE UPON A TIME	*157*
CELEBRATING THE PRINCE OF PEACE	*159*
THE LIL MISSUS	*162*

THE END

CHAPTER ONE
UTTER NONSENSE

I LONG FOR THE GOOD OLD DAYS

Way back in the good old days, when the alarm went off in the bedroom of our South Florida home, my new bride and I would leap out of bed to start another busy day. After showering, I would find her in the kitchen, basting my eggs in a quart of bacon fat. A little kiss on the neck to show my appreciation was always part of the ritual. White toast with real butter would round out the morning meal. While I ate, she would make my lunch, placing it neatly in my pail, sometimes with a secret note that she loved me.

When I got home each evening, dinner would be cooking and she would tell me about her busy day. (I swear this really happened.) I was king of my castle. Life was great. I was boss and she knew it. And when things got too hectic for us, we would run off together to this tiny, sleepy little village called Highlands, hidden in the mountains, barely in North Carolina. No one knew about this secret place.

Well, that was three children and several decades ago. Somewhere along the way a few things have changed. Oh, she still loves me, probably more now than ever. But I have lost my throne. I am no longer king. It was a slow process. I must have been too busy with heavy lifting, house repairs and football to notice that women everywhere were overthrowing men as leaders of the earth. We should have never taught them to play golf.

How could this happen, you ask? They convinced men they are always wrong. That means that women are always right. Think about it. When was the last time the little missus said, "Oh honey, you are so right, so smart and clever. Why didn't I think of that?" Men are never right anymore and I pose this serious question. "If a man speaks the absolute truth and there is no woman to hear him, is he still wrong?"

I know things have changed, not for the better, because the alarm never wakes me anymore; my bladder forces me out of bed at 6:30 each morning. I quietly gather my duds, careful not to step on that creaky spot on the bedroom floor which might wake her. Are these the actions of a king, I ask you? Now I waddle into the kitchen and drag a box of cereal from the shelf. Pouring it into a bowl, I notice it resembles the consistency of my hamster litter. While waiting for the milk to soak into the concoction, turning it a pale gray, I read the ingredients on the box, "mixed tocopherol, atopic acid, hydrog and lots of trisodium phosphate," yummy, yummy.

The problem I have is that I don't know how to get things back like it once was. Besides, everything is different, even Highlands. It's one thing to lose your throne, but my escape village is no more. Highlands is now a place, a town that everyone has found. Walk-wait lights in Highlands? Don't they have those in New York City? With timed parking and a by-pass, Highlands is growing up fast, too fast. I long for the old days. I miss the smell of bacon and eggs in the morning, a trip to the five-and-dime store on the hill on Fourth Street to buy sparklers for the kids. Gas up at the Gulf station and head for Helen's Barn where there was more activity outside in the parking lot than anything going on inside. Ah, those were the days. What's a dethroned king to do?

I can't live in South Florida because it has become a foreign land. Most of my friends have moved away and those that are left are too busy guarding their stuff. I have one friend who has a good paying job as rear gunner on a flower truck who is moving next week. I am stuck in South Florida because of the weather. I can't move to Highlands because if I do, each November my nose will stop up and stay that way until late May. Six months of not breathing is asking too much of me. Where does a dethroned king live?

Well, I think I'll move back to Mars. We came here in the first place because we were lonely and we heard that women would let us be in charge. Now all of that has changed. And there are no women on Mars and that means we will always be right, no matter what. Maybe I'll start a Highlands on Mars and invite women, if they will let us be right all the time. Yes, that's it, I thought to myself. I'll tell her when she wakes. I am outta' here. Mars never looked so good.

Hours later I took her by the hand. "I have something important to tell you, honey, so please sit down. Try not to be upset with me, but I have decided to move back to Mars." I held my breath, waiting for her response. She stared lovingly into my eyes but held her response. "Well, what do you think?" I finally asked. "All right, all right" she finally responded. "I'll cook you bacon and eggs."

RANDOM THOUGHTS

I have taken a liking to no fat potato chips and eat them all the time. Actually, they do have fat but it is called ***Olean*** which, like motor oil, is not digestible. The label on the bag warns of possible lower intestinal disruptions (they're being so polite) which, I will admit, does occur sometimes. But like any well oiled, precision machine, my "geezer" body does occasionally need an oil change and the chips provide a fun way to get all tuned up. Also, I have found a food store that will deliver the chips straight to my bathroom.

Speaking of bathrooms, I have just read an important statistic revealing there are 400 times more germs and bacteria growing on your computer mouse, keyboard and telephone than on your toilet seat. I am not quite sure what to do with this information but my first instincts make me want to move my office into the bathroom and leave the toilet seat up all the time. It needs more thought. I would also like to meet the person that did all that counting. You know it's a woman.

Want to see something scary? Get a flashlight, lie down on the kitchen floor and shine it under your refrigerator. Do this while the little missus isn't around, otherwise you will be involved in a major project which I have labeled "Getting caught looking under the refrigerator and now having to drag it away from the wall with one hand while holding a gallon spray can of 'Kills Anything' in the other hand project."

Always look under the refrigerator when she's not home, otherwise they have this uncanny sense that you are looking under there and will come running from another room and say, "Oh, good, I want to clean under there."

How do I know this? Yep, I just got caught, flashlight in hand, trying to identify a weird shaped thing all the way back against the wall. The term "I have been wanting to clean under there" translates into meaning I will do the heavy lifting while she waits with her hand on the front door knob just in case something other than the refrigerator moves, like a large black snake. They love it under there, but that's another story.

First, I swept up the chunky stuff because she couldn't bear to see it and finally, I mop up. Once that's completed, she approaches cautiously and announces "I am so glad I finally got to clean under there. But before you push it back in place, let me clean the top." Then she hands me a wet rag and announces "I'm too short." Once everything was back in place, I asked, "Are you exhausted from all that hard work?"

Later, I looked at the contents of my sweepings and must admit it looked a lot scarier under the refrigerator than lying in the dustpan. Here's my inventory: A crispy moth with a three inch wing span that, several nights ago, sent the little missus leaping from the couch to the bedroom, only touching the floor once. I also found the power bill from last October that we accused each other of losing, three petrified pieces of finely diced green pepper and one whole **Olean** potato chip, a little stale, but possibly still edible.

On to other issues. This spring, I am the most courteous driver in Highlands. Even though I have the right-of-way, I invite people to pull in front of me or, if they wish, just cut me off. If they accidentally bump my car, I apologize for being in their way.

When others blow their horn because my courtesy is delaying them, I pull over, giving them a big wave and smile. On my way, even though I am late for an important appointment, I smile and gladly pull over so everyone can pass. On my return trip, I feel sorry for the loaded down dump truck driver who is moving at crawl speed. When we get to town, I offer to buy him coffee, even though it took me an hour to get home, causing me to miss **The Soprano's**. Then, I wake up from my nightmare, realize it was all pretend. Relieved, I don my helmet and head out.

Finally, after living on this planet for well over sixty years, I just learned that turtles can breathe through their rectums, giving new meaning to the term "bad breath." I would like to have gone to my grave without that knowledge.

FOR WOMEN ONLY

Gather round, ladies, I have some wonderful news for you. Men, if you are reading this, stop now, because this is not for you. OK, that said, let me give you gals some real important inside information about men that will help you get along better with them... me... us. I am an authority on this subject because I have been one for a very, very long time.

I know that a lot of you more cynical soft tails out there think that most men are shallow, unreceptive, uncaring, uncommunicative, empty suits who are not interested in relationships and not understanding. This is simply not true. We need more from our women than just showing up naked and bringing beer and pizza. We are complex creatures who also have needs and concerns. With just a few simple acts on your part, you can transform your relationship with your Martian into heavenly bliss. Here's how.

The single most important thing you can do when dealing with the opposite sex is, at least once a year, tell him he is right. He doesn't even have to be right, just tell him he is. You will not believe what changes will occur in your man if you can learn to say, "Gosh, honey, you are right." I know it will be difficult for you to form these words and practice is necessary. I suggest you go to a men's department store, walk up to a mannequin and say "You're right" several hundred times before trying it on your man. Crossing your fingers behind your back also helps. If you are really smart, you will create a "You're Right" day for your man, where, for a full 24 hours, no matter what he says or does, you agree. If you do this, I almost guarantee you will see a remarkable change in the number of times he leaves the toilet seat up, which brings me to the next item on how to better control your man.

Here's another great idea. Issue "Leave the toilet seat up" coupons to him. What you are doing here is giving him full approval to do whatever he wants with the toilet seat. When he decides to leave it up, he merely rips a coupon from his booklet and hands it to you. You are then required to leave the seat up until its next use. Is that clever, or what?

Once all of this is accomplished, you are ready for phase two, control of the TV remote, also known as the clicker. Here, another major attitude change will be needed on your part. Giving up the remote for one hour does not mean you will lose control of the entire relationship. I recommend two remotes at first, one for each of you. Your man's remote doesn't even have to work. He just needs something to hold in his other hand while sipping his beer and watching TV.

Now, since HBO's "Sex in the City" is finally over, (Thank God) it is time for you to do a reality check on yourself and realize that we are not what that program suggested, a bunch of easily manipulated boneheads, only interested in sex, who could be controlled and cast aside as needed. What that program failed to recognize was that we would concede to all those things if we could only be right once a year.

Giving your man his own remote and telling him he is right will give him a feeling of great power. Also, tell him he never has to watch the "Lifetime" channel again, even if it is not true.

I have saved the hardest adjustment for last. Keeping your lip zipped while he is driving the car. I know you see this as his most vulnerable time and want to take full advantage of him at a time when he is concentrating on keeping you alive in heavy traffic, but avoid this temptation. I know you want to rag him over something you have strong feelings about and what better time than when he is busy and can't think of great comebacks. Instead say, "You are such a good driver. Didn't you used to drive for NASCAR?" Or better still, "This is thrilling. Try taking the curves a little faster." Stuff like that.

And finally, when you decide to present him with his own, gift wrapped, TV remote and toilet seat coupons, do so in the nude. Offer beer and pizza.

YIKES, I LOOK LIKE MY FATHER

It finally happened. I woke up, stared into the mirror and saw my father looking back at me. I am officially old. If you can remember milkmen and black and white TV, you may have already had this experience. On the day I was born, my father was already forty years old, sporting a full head of white hair and rugged facial lines which women call wrinkles.

You will be pleased to hear I did not panic. Instead, I went to the trusty Internet where there is an answer for literally everything. Using my ***"Key Word"*** feature, I typed in "wrinkles + geezer + old + white hair + looks like Father". POW, out came a myriad of answers for me to wade through and ponder. "This is great," I thought, "I don't have to look like my Father." Since going under the knife is much too frightening for me, I erased all web addresses suggesting I bleed to look younger.

FRED WOOLDRIDGE

After much study, I chose two options. The first was lip enlargement. The ad said that I could look ten years younger with injections to my skinny, almost non existent lips. I was convinced that with fat lips, I would definitely look younger. The treatment turned out to be almost painless. The next morning I stared into the mirror and found I no longer look like my father. I now look like Julia Roberts' father.

But I am a man who does not give up easily. I found a company that will super glue small, skin colored strips to your face and pull all your sagging flesh up under your hairline. Since I have short hair, which is also falling out, I opted for a Beatles type wig to hide the strips. "Awesome," I thought, as I looked into the mirror and saw a new, younger me. With fat lips, a Beatles wig and flesh stretched tight, I was a John Lennon look-a-like, only with fat lips.

There are drawbacks to my new look. My wife, who suggested that for a younger look I should have my head shrunk, will no longer be seen with me in public. After much coaxing, I finally convinced her to attend a party where only a few people knew us. I ignored the whispers about this not being a costume party and was determined to have a good time. I knew my new look was working because my friends kept congratulating the little missus on finally dumping that old codger for a younger man.

As the evening wore on my wife seemed to get more comfortable with my new look and I even forgot that I was stretched tighter than our town budget. Then it happened. My good friend, Mike, told a funny joke and, in my laughter,

I tore the holding strips on the right side of my face and everything dropped to its original place. The laughter stopped instantly as everyone stared at me in dismay. "Is that you, Fred?", Mike asked, as he stared at the right side of my face. This time I did panic and raced for my car only to find my wife was already sitting in the passenger seat, pounding her head against the dash.

We said nothing to each other all the way home. Sitting in our driveway, I finally broke the silence. "Do you think my father was a handsome man?" I asked. "Most definitely," she replied, reaching over to peel a couple of flesh strips dangling from my face. Taking that as a "Yes, I forgive you for being a bonehead" response, I leaned forward to get a kiss. "Not so fast, Wooldridge," she said as she pushed me back to my side of the car. "I told you before, no kissing until your lips deflate."

I'M OUT OF THE CLOSET!!

I can't stand the anguish any longer, the tormented feeling that is constantly on my mind; the ache in the pit of my stomach that never goes away. The fear of just letting it out is more than I can bear, but I must. I know my friends and colleagues will be so disappointed in me, but I can't take the sneaking around any longer. I'm coming out of my closet. I am publicly confessing that I love quiche.

There, I've said it. Now you can love me or hate me, depending on what your prejudices are on the male species eating quiche. I know the National Rifle Association will drop my membership and I will no longer be allowed to play in any poker game in the United States but this is something I had to do.

I have been a closet quiche eater for a long time. It happened to me in South Florida, where male quiche eaters are more acceptable than in the mountains. We were in a place called Flashback Restaurant. Since breakfast is served at any hour, I ordered the He Man Special, complete with T Bone steak, four eggs, sunny side up, and a huge bowl of grits, soaking in butter. My wife ordered a spinach quiche.

As I started my sumptuous repast, she commented on how delicious her meal was and offered a bite. "You like spinach, try this." "You must be kidding," I remarked, pushing her fork back to her side of the table. But she persisted, shoving her fork, laden with quiche, under my nose. I carefully looked around the restaurant and when I was sure that no one was looking, I quickly opened my mouth, consuming the bite.

Well, that was it. I enjoyed that one bite more than my whole He Man Special. I was hooked for life. Since then, I have been sneak-eating quiche every chance I get. When we have it at home, I always make sure the blinds are drawn. When we go out, my wife orders two quiches and I just order a beer. When no one is looking, she slides one of her two plates toward the middle of the table with the meal cut up in little bites. I take quick stabs at the food with my fork, but only when the coast is clear. Once, I was caught, red handed, shoving a large piece of broccoli quiche into my mouth. The man at the next table just shook his head in disgust. I was so embarrassed.

Things eventually got better because I found a restaurant that catered to closet quiche eaters. The chef was a master at disguising a quiche to look like something else. My favorite was the Delmonico steak, which was, in reality, a salmon, onion and cheese quiche shaped and colored to look like a steak. He even had fake steak sauce in a bottle. Once inside, I could relax, knowing that the restaurant was full of closet quiche eaters like myself. Occasionally we would make eye contact and give each other a knowing wink. It was great.

Now I don't have to worry about that anymore. I am out in the open and I don't care what your opinion of me might be. I am going to shout to the world, "I love quiche," and that really feels good. If this keeps up, I may tell you about my other closet secret, as soon as I finish the sweater.

SHE CARRIED A BIG STICK AND NEVER WALKED SOFTLY

My parents had to literally drag me, kicking and screaming, into St. Bridget's School. I was, at the age of seven, completely out of control. Not only did I manage to flunk the first grade, but I am sure the public school I attended asked my parents to take me elsewhere. If Ritalin had been invented, I would have had a permanent IV hooked to my arm.

I'll just call her Sister Watzername because I can't remember her real name, even though she was my first grade teacher and caused me to wet my bed until my twenty-second birthday. She looked like a dangerous, giant penguin. At first, I thought she didn't have hands, but later found that she liked to keep them hidden in her sleeves, along with a thick, triangular ruler.

During my first week of school, I noticed many differences between public and Catholic school. For example, in public school, they locked me in the cloak room for punishment where I would rifle through my classmates' coat pockets for lunch money, gum and baseball cards. Catholic schools also used the cloak room for punishment, except they never locked the door. That's because I was in there hanging by my thumbs from the coat rack.

There were other noted differences between the schools. During that era there were two major groups of people using the metal clicker, called a cricket; the 82nd Airborne and the sisters at St. Bridget's School. The paratroopers used the clickers to signal each other behind German lines while the Sisters used the crickets to control my thought processes. One click, stand up, two clicks, sit down, many rapid clicks, you are headed for the cloak room.

I think Sister Watzername was trained by Adolph Hitler as she had many of the same talents. Not only had she shown me the many uses of her white oak yardstick, but she seemed to know my every thought and kept ahead of me the entire year. Later, I would learn that she was getting secret reports from my former first grade teacher's psychiatrist about my behavior patterns. Not fair.

By mid year, Sister and I had come to terms and my behavior had improved. I know this because the welts on my

I'M MOVING BACK TO MARS

knuckles had almost disappeared and I hadn't visited the cloak room in weeks. I had also learned to control my bladder by the clicker. In Catholic schools, the teacher decides when it needs emptying. One click, the class stands, another click, you file out of class and head for the restrooms, girls to the left, boys to the right. Of course, not a word is spoken. Did I mention that I had to take a vow of silence before being admitted?

The pinnacle of my school year came in early spring when my class was visiting the restrooms. Sister always kept the laboratory door open about a foot, to listen for talking. I was at the urinal and noticed my best buddy was next to me. Whispering to my friend, I had momentarily forgotten she had the ears of a German shepherd.

She clicked once, signaling she heard talking. I continued and she clicked again, this time rapidly. I wanted to finish my story so I leaned sideways and was literally whispering in his ear. Little did I know she had already swung the door wide open and was standing right behind me. She was furious and for the first time, I had managed to drive this poor woman into a fit of rage. Not thinking, she swung me around and yes, you guessed it, I soaked the front of her long black garments. I will leave out the grim ending to this event, but will tell you, to this day, I cannot bring myself to speak when visiting a restroom.

My story has a happy ending, though, because I did make it to the second grade. She taught me discipline the hard way because I made her do it that way. I read and write fairly well and I am a whiz at math because she gave

FRED WOOLDRIDGE

me the basic tools to become a good learner. And what is most important, there was love, always love. Even when she and I were at our worse, I always sensed her love. God only knows what I would have become without the help of this fine, patient lady, who forced me to behave. Thank you, Sister Watzername, wherever you are.

PS- You were right, Sister, the scars did eventually disappear.

SEX

Actually this is not about sex at all, but it was the only way I could be assured that every breathing person reading this book would at least read the first paragraph. This is a story about fruitcake. If I had said that in the title, only twelve people would be reading this.

Wait; don't give up on me yet. Hidden in this article about fruitcake are the following: A tacky rumor about a well known politician, an insulting remark about a local building contractor and an inside tip about a new fast food restaurant about to open right on Main Street. Read on.

A recent study of fruitcake owners in our town has revealed that there are a whopping twelve of you out there. These owners keep their treasured cakes in their freezer until December of each year when they thaw them out and exchange them as gifts with other fruitcake lovers who immediately put their gift back in the freezer until next December. These twelve fruitcakes have been passed back and forth now for over forty years. Is that awesome?

I'M MOVING BACK TO MARS

It is believed that fruitcake was first invented by the Egyptians and rumor has it that King Tut may have a large piece still lodged in his throat, alas, causing his demise. Actually, because King Tut may have been a couple of clicks left of center, the slang term "fruitcake" may have originated. (If you believe that, I have some cheap mountain view property to sell you.) After the death of their beloved king, fruitcake disappeared until the late nineteenth century Denmark when Otto and Brun-Hilda Nackenshasher (common spelling) re-invented the dessert.

Brun-Hilda noticed that several jars of her candied fruit were past their shelf life and had turned grey. Not wanting to waste her labor of canning the fruit, she dumped the mess into a large bowl and leaned over to take a big sniff. "Vas ist los? Der is some-ding rotten here in Denmark", she screamed as she withdrew. (Now you know where that term came from.)

Next, she dumped a half bottle of schnapps on the rotting fruit and let it sit for the rest of the day. Then she announced, "Is ready. I will mix it mit mind wonderful strudel recipe and make a cake. Ve will call it 'Fruitcake'."

After cooling the cake in the window for a couple of hours, she told Otto he could have the first bite. He noticed that none of the neighborhood flies were landing on the cake and said, "No, Brun-Hilda, da pleasure is yours." "No, Otto, I insist." This went back and forth a few times until Otto spotted Brun-Hilda fingering a nearby rolling pin.

Otto chewed the first bite with a blank expression. Without swallowing, he held the remaining portion upward, trying not to gag, and declared, "Dis fruitcake is much too delicious to waste on you and I. Ve need to give this to our friends as a token of our love." Then, when Brun-Hilda wasn't looking, Otto spit the bite into his upper jacket pocket which, of course, created the ever popular term, "Fruit Pockets," currently being sold in the frozen food section of your local food stores.

The cake was wrapped with a big bow and presented to their friends, Helga and Dork Hoffenslammer, who never spoke to them again. They, in turn, were able to give the cake away the following Christmas to other friends who also never spoke to them again..

Now you know how this wonderful tradition all got started. Here's a little tip you might want to use when deciding what to do with a fruitcake given to you next Christmas. Turn the entire cake on its side and, with a large bread knife, carefully slice a thin sliver off the bottom. Then, if it tastes like Brun-Hilda's cake, you just put it in the freezer until next year when you can dump it on a friend. Is that clever, or what?

Oh yes, please forgive me for lying about the tacky hidden rumors and insults supposedly in the article. I was really desperate to get folks to read this.

CART WARS
If you go, wear protection

"There she is," I whispered to my wife. "She's the one who gave me the groin shot last week." "It was an accident. Look how old she is. Cut her some slack," the little missus

I'M MOVING BACK TO MARS

responded. "Ha," I muttered under my breath. As we slowly approached, I maneuvered my shopping cart in position to get a good glancing blow at her cart. Wham, over went her milk and a large pink bottle of **Pepto-Bismol**. I rolled by, pretending not to notice. Revenge is so sweet when it's a week old.

Each winter, thousands of tiny little women, wearing Reebok sneakers, descend on South Florida supermarkets for the cart wars. It is one of the reasons I love to come here. While my wife thinks all this occurs by accident, I happen to know some of these old gals have reputations for being the toughest and most skilled cart fighters in the land. They come to duel with the best and the cane is their weapon of choice.

One of the first things you learn as a skilled cart fighter is to never take your hands off your cart to get food. If you do, your opponent will opt to either ram your cart, sending it flying up the isle, knocking over the large display of cockroach poison, or she will take your cart two aisles over and put sixty four jars of baby food in it.

But that's amateur stuff. To be a really good cart fighter, you must be subtle with your moves, like placing your cart in the aisle so no one can get by. Then, bending down, pretending to tie your shoe, you jam wood chocks into your cart wheels. Now, step back and watch. Ramming your cart, locked in position, will send shock waves up your opponent's arms, rattling her upper plate and knocking the tease out of her hair. Score one for me.

FRED WOOLDRIDGE

Here's another great move I have mastered. First, you must pretend to be totally absorbed with looking at something on the food shelf. Then, without looking at your opponent, slowly push your cart forward, crushing her between your cart and the tomato juice display. To score a win, you must push until she complains or knocks over several cans of tomato juice. Then, look startled and smile.

I have fought with the best. Last week I knew I was in trouble when I felt a hand push against my shoulder. "Excuse me, I need to be here," she remarked as she pushed me away from cottage cheese. That is when I noticed the cane protruding out the front of her cart, like a giant lance, just the right height for groin shots. Not only had she pushed me out of cottage cheese but her cart had me pinned between my cart and chicken breasts. She was good, real good. Later, I watched her nail an old geezer with her cane that left him doubled up in pain, holding on to his cart for support.

She worked her way through the aisles, taking out one opponent after the next. She was awesome. I would have to wait patiently and make my move at just the right moment. Then, it happened. She took her eyes off her cart for just a moment and I moved in. It was one of my more subtle moves. I rolled by her, careful not to have our carts touch. Then, I followed her to the check out counter where the cashier looked on in disbelief as she rang up the oversized can of muscle building protein drink, a package of condoms and two boxes of Lucky Boy chewing tobacco I had snuck into her cart. That's a two pointer for me.

I'M MOVING BACK TO MARS

And so life is good here in South Florida. Even the food police are having fun separating cart fighters locked in standoffs. Our food police are real survivors because if they live through a two year assignment in the parking lot, they get promoted to work inside.

While Highlands, North Carolina grocery stores may have courteous and friendly employees, where even the customers are considerate and polite, they do not have cart wars. But this is good because, by the time Spring rolls around, I will be pretty banged up and in need of some healing time. I will grocery shop in the mountains, where even the slightest cart touching is considered obscene.

HOW I AVOID TERRORISTS

I am writing this column from under my bed, a place I go whenever we are in an orange alert for terrorism. Since we bought the new heavy duty bed skirt, I feel real secure under here. Why hide under the bed you ask? Ha, that's easy. In all the literature I have read concerning terrorists activities, no one has ever mentioned that they ever look under beds.

Since most terrorists snuggle in at night and sleep on sand with a rock for a pillow, they never think to look under the bed. A recent study has revealed there are only four beds in all of Afghanistan, so it's a natural place to hide. I am currently working on a new design of refrigerator/TV/Porta Potty combo that will fit under here, allowing me to survive for a long time.

FRED WOOLDRIDGE

With a little planning, I can temporarily leave my safe haven and even travel. I merely check to see which flights my two year old granddaughter is on. She flies often and the terrorists have learned to stay away from her. This small human is capable of awesome feats, like displacing six rows of passengers during a single diaper change. While flying first class, she once emptied out the whole section with her projectile vomiting. She currently holds the world record for distance for that event. Terrorists can't deal with it and have no special training for this behavior pattern.

You may not be aware, but terrorists absolutely wig out and become terrified when they see an unclothed woman. I have not figured this out yet but it might have something to do with Middle Eastern women never disrobing or exposing anything except their eyeballs. Where is Freud when I need him? I think our Government should use more nude women in combating terrorism. For example, if all the women on a hijacked flight disrobed, the terrorists may panic and jump from the aircraft. The possibilities are endless.

Anyway, I had a plan to use this phobia to my advantage. I had just finished painting a large sign for the front yard which read "Warning, nude women nearby" when the little missus spotted it drying in the garage. This went over like a motorcycle rally at the country club and the sign is currently in my garbage can, if anyone wants it.

When I have to run to the store, I put my blow up doll, Mustang Sally, a relic from college days, in the passenger seat to keep the bad guys away. While I will admit to having

I'M MOVING BACK TO MARS

been pulled over by the police several times, I have not been assaulted by any terrorists, so the plan is working.

Sometimes I spot a person who may look like a terrorist but I am not sure. Just because he smells like a goat, has olive skin and is wearing clothes that Goodwill would throw away, does not make him a terrorist. (Actually, a couple of my friends fit that description.) This is called profiling and is prohibited in this country.

I always check for fuses protruding from their persons. The more fuses I count, the less chance that a profiling accusation will be lodged against me. The main thing I remember is not to panic. Just start looking for nearby beds. But if the fuses are lit, then a profiling accusation could become a moot issue. In this case, I usually do panic, running at top speed.

Terrorists do not drink alcoholic beverages, so if I spot a suspect terrorist, I offer him a libation. If he refuses, he becomes suspect, even though he could be a minister from a local parish. Then, I offer him a humus sandwich and if he accepts, I run. I never fully trust anyone who eats humus sandwiches anyway. Have you tasted that stuff? No wonder they want to blow themselves up.

Should you decide to adopt my plan for avoiding terrorists, let me remind you that they are ruthless and will do anything to be with twenty virgins in the afterlife, none of which, I can assure you, will be from the Miami area. Obviously, they have not thought this out. What does one do with twenty virgins anyway?

Just remember one thing. If a suspect terrorist invites you to a party, telling you it will be a real blast, head for the bed.

NEVER TRUST A MAN WHO........

My Pa used to say, "Never trust a man who looks you square in the eye and says, 'I'm just a poor ole country boy looking to make a buck' ". "If that ever happens", he continued, "grab your wallet and run." Not sure why he told me that, but he was an authority on the topic.

My Pa was born in 1896 at a small place called Upton, in Hardin County, Kentucky, just a stone's throw from where the Hatfield's and McCoy's used to shoot it out regularly. My Pa was an authentic, bona fide, poor ole country boy. 1896 was the same year Henry Ford invented his first gasoline motor car, the "Quadricycle," and drove it through the streets of Detroit.

Things were not as exciting at Pa's house. He lost both his parents to consumption (TB) before his second birthday and lived with his dirt farmer grandparents in a small, rundown farmhouse with no electricity or indoor plumbing. As soon as he could walk, he helped in the fields and by the time he reached the eighth grade, his grandparents decided he should stop wasting time in school and go to work in the coal mines.

Even though the L & N Railroad had come to Hardin County, bringing in electricity, indoor water, and other luxuries, my Pa, now sixteen, packed his stuff in a single suitcase and, with no money in his pocket, headed for Louisville, Kentucky.

General Foods Corporation was expanding rapidly and looking for traveling salesmen to sell their products. By this time, Henry Ford had perfected the Model T and was selling them to whomever could afford one. General Foods had just bought six coupes to assign to newly hired salesmen. At the job interview, the company asked my Pa about his background. He looked them square in the eye and told them he was just a poor ole country boy looking to make a buck. They hired him instantly.

Pa couldn't have been happier. He went all the way from dirt farming to cruising around in a brand new Model T and getting paid for it. Each Monday morning, Pa would load up his coupe with catalogs and food supplies, mostly cereal, and head out across the State, returning with an empty car and a fist full of money. When skeptical purchasers would give a leery glance, he would look them square in the eye and tell them, "I'm just a poor ole country boy looking to make a buck." During his evening stops, he would dazzle the young ladies with his music by playing the hand saw with his bow.

By the time I was born, Pa had given up his traveling salesman job and was delivering milk. He eventually saved enough to buy a restaurant, then another. I would question him about his traveling days, looking for juicy stories of a single man on the road. But my Pa was never my friend; he was my Pa. Telling me stories of the old days would bring us much too close for his comfort.

The only story I ever got from him was he claimed to have invented "Postum", a cereal substitute that Pa would deliver to the Kentucky State Prison on a weekly basis. Pa went to his grave complaining he had been cheated out of his invention. Since Postum was invented the same year Pa was born, it could be he had bumped his head on the field plow one too many times.

Although I'll never know for sure, I would like to think that Pa was a poor ole country boy who could be trusted. He raised three kids, only married once, living with my Ma until he died. I never once saw him do a dishonest thing and never heard him say one single curse word, not even "damn" after striking his thumb with a hammer. He thought all people who went to church were hypocrites, treated black people like chattel and worked sixteen hours a day right up until the end of his life. Not once did I ever see him pray.

But since Pa wasn't dealt many good life cards, I'm hoping God took that into consideration and eventually let him into heaven. If so, there has to be a special place, maybe over in the corner, for Hardin County poor ole country boys who were just looking to make a buck.

BYE BABY BUNTING
FRED'S GONE A HUNTING

Saws have stopped buzzing, hammers are quiet and closed storefront signs are appearing everywhere. The rich can't get their houses built and if your car needs fixing, it will just have to wait. Hunting season is here and the

I'M MOVING BACK TO MARS

testosterone is flowing through the male species by the gallon. The driving need to shoot something is insatiable. It's a time for male bonding, camp fires, bad jokes and snuff.

I am embarrassed to tell you that I am not a game hunter and never have been. Here in the mountains it is hard not being a hunter because that is all everyone talks about for months. "How many points did it have?" is the commonly asked question. I thought everyone was talking about playing bridge.

So this season, I decided to hunt. Since I know nothing about shooting critters, I hired a professional to take me hunting. We will just call him Dilbert because, after our hunting experience, he said if I mention his name, he would strap antlers to my head and turn me loose in the woods. Besides, his real name rhymes with Dilbert.

On my first day of training, we had to sight in our rifles. This is done by driving to a rock quarry and setting up empty beer bottles that Dilbert finished for breakfast. Then we shoot into the granite face and try to break the bottles and dodge the ricocheting bullets at the same time.

By two o'clock the next morning we were heading for the woods. If we wanted to find vacant trees, we would have to get an early start as it was the first day of hunting season and virtually every tree would have a hunter in it by daybreak. Armed with my loaded rifle, one extra bullet, a flask of Jack Daniels and a tin of snuff, I was raring to go.

Since deer never look up, all the hunters hide up in their tree stands. Some of the more experienced hunters put their tree stands up the day before and tack "no vacancy" signs to their trees. It took us awhile to find a couple of vacant trees but finally we got snuggled in. Sitting in a tree stand in the pitch black was a little boring, but Dilbert said to be patient and the fun would soon begin. This is when my sneezing attacks started. I must have been allergic to something in my tree. Each time I would sneeze, scores of hunters would shush me. I was just getting my sneezing under control, when I accidentally knocked my rifle off my tree stand. As fate would have it, the gun went off when it struck the ground. This brought on a chorus of expletives from the other hunters which usually would only be heard in an NFL locker room. Once I had retrieved my rifle, I settled back into my stand to await daybreak.

After a couple of sips from my flask, I was beginning to feel real seasoned. I was pumped. As daybreak came, I decided to try the snuff. I had never experienced snuff and looked forward to it. Just a little pinch between my cheek and gum and immediately I began to wheeze out of control. I spit out the mess but the wheezing continued. It was already light out and that is when I noticed that all my fellow hunting buddies had their rifles trained on my tree. I called for Dilbert, between wheezes, but he was busy pounding his head against his tree. I thought it might be best if I leave and Dilbert agreed. As I left the woods alone, I shouted "I am not a deer" and took my hat off so everyone could see I did not have antlers. Fortunately, I made it out with only a couple of firearms trained in my direction.

So I guess hunting is not for everyone, and besides, as a retired lawman, I did get to hunt humans for a long time. That was much more thrilling anyway, as many of them were

I'M MOVING BACK TO MARS

cunning and some even shot back.

Oh, I almost forgot. When I hike in the woods now, I always look up, just in case Dilbert is out there.

TRAFFIC ENFORCEMENT IS DIFFERENT

No Shooting Zones are working

I am writing from beautiful South Florida, a suburb of Cuba. If you're wondering why I would leave my secure home in the mountains to write in such a scary place, speak with my psychiatrist. Anyway, my doors are locked, the alarm is set and there's a loaded gun in every room. Besides, this will be an exciting assignment and I want to give our readers who have never visited South Florida some insight into what life is like, just in case they wig out and are thinking about moving.

The first thing you notice is the vast difference in the way traffic laws are enforced compared to my summer home. Driving the freeways in South Florida is similar to driving in Atlanta. Everyone is zipping along at eighty, cell phones in hand, with a whopping six inch space between you and the car in front. If you spot a police car, you know he has accidentally made a wrong turn and is looking for an exit to get off before he gets hurt. But Atlanta just can't compete with South Florida when it comes to traffic shootouts.

In Highlands, police take traffic enforcement serious. Speeding around at thirty nine miles per hour will eventually land you a traffic citation. This system works well because citizens learn the police are serious about traffic enforcement and everyone, except those dumb as toast, drive near the speed limit. If Highlands officers ever decide to crack down on walk/don't walk violators, the increased revenue could lower taxes dramatically. Also, Highlands' police really get their shorts in a wad if there's a traffic shootout.

But down here, things are different. If you are spotted by police while involved in a traffic shootout, you are definitely getting pulled over. If this is your first offense, though, you will get a warning. But if you have been stopped before for blazing away at your fellow motorist, you'll get ticketed. One exception to this is getting caught in a gun battle in a posted "No Shooting Zone," usually around schools and parks. Not only will you get a ticket, but your firearm will be confiscated for a full twenty four hours. This no nonsense policy has really impacted the area as gun play in "No Shooting Zones" is down dramatically. No one wants to be here without their firearm.

If you are pulled over for a traffic violation, the officer will ask you for your license, parole officer's name, passport and gun permit. He will say this in four languages, including Arabic, so don't try the old "no peekee inglés" trick.

In Highlands, displaying suspicious behavior during a traffic stop may result in the officer asking you to open your trunk. This will never happen down here. The fear for the officer is that he will either find a dead body or a trunk full of cocaine. A recent survey has shown there are more motorists riding around South Florida with dead bodies in their trunks than anywhere. In either case, the officer will be facing countless hours of paper work and overtime, something he has too much of already. He would like to go home to his family once in awhile.

Another wonderful thing they have here is "meter station" parking. It's kind of a game you play with the cops. Once parked (ha), you exit your vehicle and race to an automated meter station a half block away to buy a timed parking permit. The challenge is to return to your car before the officer writes you a ticket. Then, you realize you don't have the right change for the meter station and you now race two more blocks to find a store that is willing to make change. Merchants are as testy about giving change as merchants in Highlands are about tourists using their restrooms. By the time you get back to your car, there's a ticket on your windshield. Like most Floridians, you will put this ticket in your glove compartment along with several hundred other tickets you haven't paid.

I know my column has made you antsy to get down here, but let me caution you not to come. There are many Middle Easterners here taking flying lessons and if the police spot one with dynamite strapped on him, they become anxious and nervous, closing the highways, sometimes for hours, even days. You may never get here. Worse yet, you may never get out. My advice is to stay put.

SQUIRREL LOVERS, TAKE A PROZAC

I had not told a soul, but now it's time for people to know. If you are a squirrel lover, stop and read no further, or take a Prozac.

FRED WOOLDRIDGE

Five years ago, I found a way to defeat squirrels (and bears) from eating my bird seeds. This is 100% foolproof. I was proud of myself but kept it quiet because I figured I could patent this idea and be a millionaire overnight, or at least make enough to pay my taxes. Squirrels are going hungry around my place and I say, "Let them eat cake." Companies spend thousands on research, trying to design feeders that are squirrel-proof. This is serious business, but none of them work and the squirrels always win, until now.

In my back yard, I have a large tree with a high, horizontal limb. I purchased a large spool of heavy duty weed eater filament and attached the end onto an arrow I swiped from my grandson. SWOSH, I shot the arrow over the limb and the line followed. Attaching my favorite feeder to the line I pulled it up to a point it was suspended in mid air, fifteen feet from the trunk of the tree. Squirrels are good jumpers, but no critter was going to try a fifteen foot leap high above the ground. Score: Fred 1 Squirrels 0

For the past three years I have sat on my deck and watched the birds eat safely from my squirrel proof feeder. Squirrels, also known as tree rats, came and went. They stomped their little feet in frustration. They barked at the feeder and made weird, obnoxious sounds as they ran up and down the trunk of the tree. Then they would leave. Remembering the hundreds of pounds of bird seed squirrels had consumed over the years, I sat on my deck and cheered, making hand gestures at them that I learned while driving in Miami.

I'M MOVING BACK TO MARS

This spring, I fired my line over the limb and in minutes was set up and ready to relax. Then Wallenda arrived. That's what I call him, a young boomer who is braver than the famous Flying Wallenda trapeze artist and tight rope walker of yesteryear. Wallenda leaped from the trunk of the host tree and started his journey through space toward the feeder, barely grabbing it with one front foot. The feeder spun violently, but Wallenda had achieved what no other critter had. He was scarfing down my seeds.

Score: Fred 1   Wallenda 1

In shock, I leaped to my feet, flung my hands in the air, and growled louder than when people complain about my column. Wallenda panicked, leaped from the feeder but was not able to reach the tree. He fell and hit the ground hard with a loud thump. "Ha," I thought, "that hurt; he won't be back." Minutes later, Wallenda was back and made another spectacular leap from the tree to the feeder. I sat in astonishment. What's worse, Wallenda was unfazed by his hard fall each time he visited the feeder. By the end of the week, the score was: Wallenda - 30   Fred - 1.

Rummaging through my stuff in the basement, I came across my old yellow snake that I used to scare my grandkids with. Rubber mouth wide open with a red forked tongue, it was a very scary reptile. Wallenda watched me lower the feeder to the ground. The snake fit perfectly on the top of the feeder. I pointed to him, "You are toast," I said. It only took the birds a few minutes to realize the snake was a fake and continued to feed. But Wallenda stomped his feet, barked at the snake and ran up and down the tree, making weird, obnoxious noises with his mouth. He was afraid to make the leap right into the jaws of my snake. Game is over, Fred wins.

And the best news of all is that I am almost ready to open my new business. I will call it Fast Freddie's Friendly Feeder Franchise. Squirrels, go get a life someplace else. I will open as soon as my box of rubber snakes arrives.

I'M HOPPING MAD AT HOMOSEXUALS

Last year I boldly came out of my closet and announced to the world that I love quiche. I paid dearly for saying that because I can no longer be a member of the NRA and every poker game in America has banned me from their game, simply because I love quiche, especially with spinach and cheese.

Well, here I go again, getting myself in big time trouble. I am currently mad at homosexuals. There, I said it. Get over it. Don't get your shorts in a wad because I have a right to be mad.

Just so you'll know, I am a heterosexual person. It was never a choice I had to consciously make. My genes dictated that I would be this way. Simply put, I am attracted to members of the opposite sex and I make no apologies. I assume the attraction for the same sex is comparable for gay folks. If saying that disturbs you, then you may be "heterophobic", a term I just made up which is a fear or aversion to non gay folks.

I'M MOVING BACK TO MARS

What homosexual people do with their lives is none of my business. I say let the man upstairs sort it all out when we all hopefully get there. Sure our life styles are different and I say "Oh well." Besides, this has nothing to do with why I'm mad anyway.

I am hopping mad because gays have robbed me of some of my favorite clichés and have made me alter my lifestyle accordingly. It was so much easier on us "straight" guys (that's what they call us) when homosexuals were all nicely squirreled away in their closets and we didn't have to think about all of this. But that's history. Now, homosexuality is "in your face" and I have had to make adjustments that I don't like. Now that everyone is out of the closet on everything, I boldly announce I love being heterosexual. I want to act like a "straight" and do "straight" things even though the term is something I am not comfortable with. That's part of why I'm mad. I don't like being called "straight." It just doesn't fit who I am.

There's more. Now that we are all out of whatever closet we were in, I have had to go through my closet (ha) and throw out all my gay apparel. I used to take great pleasure during the Christmas season donning my gay apparel and singing "Fa la la la la la la la la." In this new century, only a gay person would sing "Fa la la la la la la la la." I miss doing that.

Since "gay" has become the acceptable word to describe homosexuals, I can no longer have a gay time or say "We were happy and gay." Thank goodness I am not a caballero or I would be even more upset.

In a simpler time, I could hang out with gay friends without everyone whispering "I'll bet he's homophobic and just trying to compensate." What does that mean? Now, I am self conscious and feel like I have to start each sentence with "My wife and I..." Before, it never mattered. I am also mad because now that homosexuality is out in the open, there seems to be a "us and them" mentality.

It gets worse. In my other life as a cop, I had a partner. He was not gay although the department had several. Outside of your immediate family, your partner is the next most important person in your life. You are literally responsible for each other's life.

That brings on an unconditional loyalty that few people understand. Because gay folks now have "partners" I can no longer put my arms around my partner, give him a big hug and tell him I still love him. At least not in public because I will get strange looks from all my straight, homophobic friends when I smile and announce "He is my partner."

Before gays adopt words to describe what or who they are, they should think about us poor straight guys and gals who might have to suffer with that decision. They have already grabbed up words like "bear", "wolf", "daddy", "chaser" and, my all time favorite "friend of Dorothy." All I ask is that they please, please, please don't create a cliché called "friend of Fred" which, of course, would mean "A sick puppy."

I'M MOVING BACK TO MARS

IS BEING DEAD LIKE HOLDING YOUR BREATH FOREVER?

This is my take on what it's like to be dead. By tomorrow morning, all 371 pastors and our only Catholic priest living in the Highlands area will probably be mad at me. They will join the ever growing list of members of the "Mad at Fred" club which, just to mention a few, include building contractors, deer hunters, snooty people, Buckheaders, Miamian's, cops, homosexuals, ya de, ya de, ya de.

It was a standup comedian who said being dead was like holding your breath forever. I sure hope he was wrong because I hate doing that. I always came in last place at Camp Pee-a-ming-o in the "sit on the bottom of the pool" contest. I will make a lousy dead person if I have to hold my breath.

I am certain that my third grade teacher, Sister Whachamacallit, was wrong when she said, "Child, you are going straight to the fires of hell, where the flames are so hot that a spoonful of molten lava will taste cool on your lips." I had just been caught eating a bologna sandwich on a Friday. Because of her, I no longer eat bologna sandwiches at all. It was about that same time I came to realize that life was not fair. There are the have and have nots. Some get off easy, some struggle. There are the smart and dumb, bad and good, people who are allowed to eat bologna sandwiches and those who can't. People do get away with murder and we are not created equal.

Life is puzzling because bad things always seem to happen to good people. If you ask a man of the cloth about this he will probably say "The Lord works in mysterious ways" which, of course means "I don't have a clue."

After I grew up, I rationalized that our Creator is probably not too hung up on bologna sandwiches on Friday. Besides, eating bologna sandwiches is currently way down on my list of stupid stunts I have pulled since the third grade.

Here is another issue I struggle with. I once knew a black man, born into the world with absolutely nothing going for him, which included being born black in the sixties. Way below average in intelligence, he made his way through life as best he could. His mom was a hooker and his dad just one of her customers passing through town. The main influence in his life was his mom's pimp who had him running dope by the age of 12. By the of age 28, they were strapping him into an electric chair for killing a cop.

I wonder what fate met this man in death. Will he be judged harshly for his crimes on earth and be punished even further or will he be at peace? How does he stack up in death with the guy across town, born with wealth and intelligence, who had everything going for him and lived a good religious life? The answer, of course, is "The Lord works in ..." oops, I mean I don't have a clue and neither does anyone else."

I have learned this much. It is so easy **not** to be prejudiced if you have never been exposed to prejudice; to love everyone if you have not been hated by someone; to be a good person when you are surrounded with all things good, and to be bad and evil if that is all your life has been. In death, I believe God will sort this all out in a fair manner which, hopefully,

I'M MOVING BACK TO MARS

will not include the eating of bologna sandwiches.

Life is a mystery to me because I can't figure out why it has to be so cruel and unfair for some and so wonderful for others. I just hope there is not reincarnation as I am sure to wind up as Omar Khadafy's pet goat.

Finally, I have had to conclude, while life is unfair, death is not. Death just has to be the great equalizer, where the rich and poor, bad and good, all come together with one thing in common: they are all dead. Death cannot be as judgmental, cruel and unfair as life.

And I am still troubled with Sister Whachamacallit's comments on the bologna sandwich. Do you think she could have been right?

FRED'S THEORY OF EVOLUTION

(Darwin was a monkey's uncle.)

I am allowed to trash Charles Darwin and his theories on evolution because he is dead and the poor guy can't defend himself. Anyway, that is what we like to do. We wait until a person is dead, then we either make him a hero, a saint or a legend or we dismember him piece by piece, along with his research. Sometimes, as in Darwin's case, we first make him a hero and legend, and then we dismember him.

There are many reasons to be skeptical of Charlie boy. First, he is a Brit, born in Kent in the early eighteen hundreds. People really talked funny in those days and could not be trusted. They said weird things like "Thou woust, thou coust" when asked if they would like passage to the Galapagos Islands.

Secondly, never trust a man from Kent. You know about the poem, "There once was a man from Kent." That alone makes me nervous and it gets worse. Darwin got to go to the Galapagos Islands only if he promised to entertain the Captain during the long days at sea. Hmmm, what does that mean?

And there is good reason to believe that Charles may have been a couple of clicks left of center. I say this with credibility because he did not take the "woman" species with him. It is a known fact that man cannot exist for too long without the "woman" species. All your systems kind of get stopped up and the brain eventually begins to malfunction. These malfunctions are sometimes called sperm headaches.

This is probably why he got a little squirrelly right in the middle of his research. I have not been to those islands, but if I did go, I would definitely bring the little missus with me, just so I wouldn't start creating weird theories and look at bugs and other critters with my microscope.

Now that I have thoroughly disproved the Darwin theory by trashing his reputation, let me tell you how it really happened. Although I am still not certain that building contractors did not descend from snails, I am going to stick my neck out and give you the real poop (Excuse my language.) on how it all happened.

Once upon a time, millions and millions of years ago, on a planet far, far away, the king of Karputchecupiania

I'M MOVING BACK TO MARS

(common spelling) made a proclamation. "I am sick and tired of being sick and tired. Round up all our misfits, which shall include lawyers, quack doctors who like to 'practice' on their patients, CEO's, money grabbing investors, satire writers, car salesmen and real estate agents."

"Send them to that obscure little planet in the corner of the galaxy we call Earth and let them live with the other illiterate critters that are already there. Also ship a few apple trees so they won't starve right away and make sure they are naked. I don't want anyone finding them and identifying them as Karputchecupianians. For once, we will have some peace and quiet around here."

So there you have it. The space ship landed at a small oasis somewhere around Iraq or Turkey and dumped the misfits and the apple trees. After sitting there staring at each other for about ten minutes, they did what any group of misfits would do, they began fighting. There were instant splinter groups. The CEO's and investors banded together against the car and real estate salesmen, who were trying to figure out ways to beat the doctors and lawyers out of their money. The satire writers tried to stay neutral and wrote funny stories about all the splinter groups. These writings later became known as bibles.

The King of K was so pleased with his decision, he later sent other misfits to planet Earth. There were rogues, scalawags and vagabonds who later became moon shiners, insurance salesmen and poets. They also sent us Hare Krishna people with orders to hang out in airports and bus terminals and get us to join them so that we can also smoke those skinny cigarettes that make you not care you are a misfit.

Is it any wonder we are this way, a planet of misfits, trying to grab all the money we can get our hands on before we die so we can pass it on to our misfit children who will do the same? That's my theory and I'm sticken' to it. Feel free to trash it once I'm dead.

VOO-DOO BRIDGE

I am writing to all those wonderful people who are **not** yet addicted to a card game called bridge. I think there are at least five of you left. Congratulations on your perseverance in keeping the "four no trump" needle out of your arm.

As for me, I'm a goner. The little missus and I have been mainlining since the sixties and became addicted way back when our entire paychecks were divided between the mortgage company and the grocery store. We bought an inexpensive deck of cards and the rest is history. Nowadays it seems that folks are addicted to much harsher substances than bridge which, I am sure, cost more than a deck of cards.

Being the out of control person I am, I have never played well, mostly because I have the attention span the length of a black bear eating your bird seeds. But everything is about to change. I have found a way to level the field. Standby, bridge players, here I come.

I'M MOVING BACK TO MARS

I have just finished the arduous task of designing miniature replicas of every single bridge player I know. Most of my dolls are lifelike, have serious faces, oversized fannies, complete with calluses and you know why. I have had to do this to survive as my fellow players are a sinister bunch and most play better than I.

Just before a bridge game, I select the dolls of the players I know will show up. A hot needle in the neck always does the trick. Harsher measurers are sometimes needed, like for the guy who always comes out in first place, a poke in the eye will send him reeling. And for that lady who always leans over and asked "How long have you been playing bridge?" a jolt to her calluses will work nicely.

I know my system is working because all my bridge buddies arrive for play complaining of stiff necks, headaches and sore derrieres. Sometimes I bring a few dolls with me, just in case they need a second stab. I excuse myself and head for the restroom. Once I have secreted myself in a stall, I break out the dolls and stab away. I can sometimes hear the shrieking from all the way down the hall.

Once the game begins we are a serious bunch. We start by speaking in codes and never smile, especially when we are in the throws of battle. If a bridge player does smile, he has gas. Couples develop plans of attack and plot schemes to win. Even when we gather in small rooms of forty and fifty people, there is still no talking.

There is also a game called "silent bridge" where even the secret codes are not spoken. Total silence is a must.

When I go, the little missus places duct tape over my mouth so we won't be thrown out. I have managed to be thrown out of these games anyway, once for developing uncontrollable hiccups with strange noises coming from my nose and another time for knocking the secret code box on the floor, spilling the codes into a mess. I have been reported to the CIA for that infraction. I am currently working on a special set of dolls that have removable brains, just for my silent bridge buddies. I will also bring a special code card with me that says, "I have to go to the restroom."

Well, got to go now 'cause my bridge game is about to start and I haven't even soaked my calluses yet.

BEWARE OF CON MEN LIKE ME!

I have just repainted the old iron bridge which crosses the Chattooga River and I'm letting it go for a song. Cash only, please. Not interested, you say? Then how about this? You give me all the cash you got in the bank and I will triple your money by tomorrow morning. As collateral for your savings, I will sign over my deed to the old iron bridge.

Con guys have been around for centuries. Actually the words "Con Man", pure and simple, is male bashing, at its best, as there are an equal amount of "Con Babes" out there plying their trade on the unsuspecting public.

In a major city that I cannot mention for fear that crooked politicians will fly up from Miami and get me, a voluptuous lady rings your door bell and informs you that she can replace your entire roof for $999. She does this while putting her

I'M MOVING BACK TO MARS

hand on your leg. If you are dumb enough to bite, she gets a modest deposit of fifty bucks and gives you an impressive contract and receipt. In one old neighborhood with lots of bad roofs, this lady netted twelve hundred bucks in one afternoon. Of course, the roofers never arrived but it was worth the money for the suckers to get a learning experience, plus a hand on their leg. Hardly anyone called the police as they were too embarrassed.

If you think for one minute that because you live out of Miami, you are safe from con men, think again. One guy I know well takes unsuspecting tourists out and fleeces them of their hard earned money by convincing them that jumping from a cliff with a rope attached, into the abyss, is a good thing. Is that scary or what?

But these people cannot hold a candle to the real con guys, the real pros who sneak into your home at dinner time and assault you when you are most vulnerable, when you are hungry. They are called tele-marketers. These silver tongued con artists are the best of the best, especially the time-share sharks.

How about a free, all expense paid weekend, including meals, in wonderful Gatlinburg, Tennessee where you will be conned into buying a two week visit each year in a hot, stuffy condo, with a view of the tattoo shops, for only $200,000? Maintenance fees are a mere $395 a month, not including property taxes and special assessments. These guys are making a fortune and they're everywhere. If I could just find their buyers, I would sell them my bridge.

What's really fun, though, is when the con guys call my house. I wait patiently and allow them to give me their whole spiel. When I am sure they are finished I say "Wow, that sounds really great. I want to sign up, but let me turn off my dinner so it doesn't burn." I lay the phone down next to some elevator music and get on with my life.

You will be amazed at how long these suckers will wait for you to come back. Sometimes, when the guy is real patient and I need to use the phone, I get back on to inform him that I sell cemetery lots in Gatlinburg and if he could give me his credit card number, I would put a lot in his name. As an added bonus, he gets to stay longer than two weeks. They usually hang up on me. Seriously now, when was the last time you had a tele-marketer hang up on you? If you were to ask me if I ever feel guilty about this behavior, I would say, no, except when they send money for the cemetery lot.

I must go now as my flight to Puerto Rico is leaving soon. I have just won an all-expense paid ski trip and I am dashing off to collect. I am bringing my iron bridge deed, just in case I find a sucker on the slopes. If you decide to buy my bridge, give me a call before I leave and I'll come by and put my hand on your leg.

DON'T BE SHOCKED, MY MENU HAS CHANGED

If you have not seen the old space movie "2001 Space Odyssey" rent it immediately as this is exactly where we are all heading. In the movie, space travelers have the ability to

I'M MOVING BACK TO MARS

chit-chat with their friendly computer, Hal, who is running the entire spacecraft but responds to voice commands from humans. Eventually, Hal flips out, takes over the ship, making his own decisions, resulting in everyone's demise.

If you are old enough, you will remember the first telephone answering machine, a crude gizmo which operated with cassette tapes but got the job done. Then along came digital gadgets, followed by the currently popular computerized answering machine used today by most institutions. "Please select from one of the following forty two options. Listen carefully as our menu has changed." Sound familiar? I am convinced that in another twenty years, there will be a "Hal" in everyone's home.

Trying to keep up with the Joneses, I have gone to great expense to buy the latest state of the art computerized answering machine for my home. I call her "Gertrude" after an old secretary who was just as grouchy and bossy as my machine. My old Gertrude had a sign on her desk which read, "Thank you for not breathing while I smoke." My new machine may be just as arrogant.

Here is how she works. When you call my house, Gertrude does not permit me to answer, even if I am home. She is real fussy about that and you will only make the mistake of answering once because an electric shock is released into your ear, magnetizing every filling in your head, making it difficult to get utensils and other metal objects out of your mouth. People with metal plates in their heads should not buy this system.

FRED WOOLDRIDGE

Anyway, callers will first hear a welcome statement by a James Cagney impersonator who says, "You dirty rat, you call my house when I am busy. I'll get you for this." If this does not get the caller to hang up, Gertrude continues. "If you are selling something, press 'one' now as I am definitely interested." Gertrude then puts the caller into a lock mode. Any attempt by the salesman to hang up will, of course, result in an electric shock to his outer ear, magnetizing his fillings. I know of salesmen who have been on hold for days.

If the caller is not a salesman, my answer machine will say, "If you are calling from a touch tone phone, press 'two' now. If not, press 'three'." Then Gertrude says, "For voice identification, say the following words, "Fred is the nicest guy on the planet". My computer then searches through a myriad of voice identifications. Voices of creditors, subscribers calling to complain about my column, distant relatives who want to visit and persons who talk longer than two minutes are put in lock mode and are eventually zapped.

For persons who don't fit into any of those categories, my machine says, "Please select from one of the following four options. If you want to borrow money, press one now." Pow, lock mode, zap. Gertrude continues. "If you have some real nasty gossip to spread, press 'two' now." This will cause Gertrude to go into "ah ha" mode, saying that and "tell me more" every thirty seconds. When the caller tries to hang up..., yep, you got it, another electrical zap to ear.

Gertrude continues, "If you have free NFL tickets for tonight's game, press 'three' now and hold while I find out

I'M MOVING BACK TO MARS

where your good buddy is. He always speaks highly of you." And finally, the machine announces, "For all other calls, press 'four' now." This will send the caller back to the James Cagney impersonator welcome message and the process is repeated.

My system is working well as I currently have twenty two calls on perpetual hold and have not received one worthwhile message. I know that eventually I will land some free NFL tickets.

One small problem. I just returned home to find that Gertrude had somehow locked me out of the house. Apparently, she had overheard a conversation with a friend where I compared her to my old secretary.

I am now on my way to the florist to buy flowers. That never worked with my old secretary and probably won't work with my answering machine. Maybe I'll call the house and apologize.

SHE IS THE CZAR OF ONE WORD SENTENCES

The directive came right from the top. "Provide safety and care of subject, returning in original condition on the same day. As always, should you accept this assignment, you are on your own."

There was a tactical briefing where plans were laid out and weapons were issued. In my arsenal were throwaway diapers with no pins, handy wipes instead of wash cloths, gas mask for diaper changes, ear plugs, tippy cup, which my wife is threatening to buy for me, and last, a handbook on how to communicate with this species.

Also included was a six pack of Doctor Seuss books and survival beer for me. Kids at two are the czars of one word sentences so the handbook is invaluable. An interesting study because, with one word commands, these small creatures are able to get adults, ten times bigger then they are, to run around like idiots. Actually, we adults should learn this communication system as it would save us all a lot of time. Here is what I learned.

When Callie calls out "stuck" this means to call the plumber because she has just shoved her head between the pipes under the sink and can't get out. Since this happens once a week, the plumber is on retainer and his phone number is in the speed dialer. When she calls out "hot" you better come quick because every burner on the range is on the high setting, melting the empty pot I left there and setting aflame my "How to Communicate with a Two Year Old" handbook.

Then there is the ever famous "no" command, which means, "I am in control here, even though you are bigger." It is also important to know that this command is meaningless when given by an adult.

The morning started with a one hour crying session because mommy wasn't there, but once I was able to control my tears, the day started to get better. During the second hour, Callie took over the crying and nothing I did seemed to work until I remembered she uses one word sentences. A

I'M MOVING BACK TO MARS

loud "stop" worked perfectly.

I fed her breakfast on the porch and, when finished, hosed everything down, including Callie. Next, play time, where she emptied my shaving cream can on the dog, a cocker that is so old and helpless, it gave up retreating a long time ago. When finished, the dog, whose breath usually smells worse than Saddam Hussein's, smelled great.

After a two hour session of dragging out every single toy in her play box and throwing it at me, it was time for lunch. That's when the idea hit me. I would feed her lunch in the front yard and I wouldn't have to hose off the porch afterwards. The whole mess would just kind of soak into the grass. This worked great until the cops arrived and I spent the next half hour explaining why I was hosing down a helpless toddler, trapped in a high chair.

Finally, the best part of the day. Callie and I are programmed to take our naps at exactly the same time, except she woke up first and seized upon the opportunity to dump baby powder all over my body. In the old days, this would call for corporal punishment, but now we use something called "time out," a totally meaningless gesture which leaves the child unpunished and the parent without guilt.

After several more misbehaviors and time outs, I reverted back to something from my Catholic school days and hung Callie by her thumbs in the closet. She really didn't like that at all, but she was an angel the rest of the day. Callie and I survived each other and, except for her thumbs, I returned her in mint condition. I never told my daughter that it was not until late afternoon that I spotted the unused gas mask sitting on the counter. If she finds out about this, I will be in "time out" for a month.

I thought Callie was saying "sticky" all day and I kept wiping her hands, when in fact she was saying "stinky" and you know what that means. Gas mask or not, I have never seen anything so horrifying in my life. Next time I get this assignment, I will not be so quick to call the plumber.

DON'T MESS WITH MY THREE LEGGED TREE RAT

(A squirrelly tail from long ago.)

We were just sitting down to dinner when we heard a loud "bang" in the back yard. The house darkened, giving our three children the opportunity to quickly bury their broccoli under their napkins. "Don't move, I'll check it out," I commanded.

There, lying at the base of our power pole in the backyard was a dead tree rat wearing his designer outfit. He had short circuited our transformer, blowing off a hind leg in the process. Then, in an instant, as if God himself had said, "Return to life, little three legged tree rat and make this family miserable", the critter began to breathe.

By this time, all three kids, disobeying my command to stay put, were leaning over me for a better look. "Quick, get that old aquarium from your closet." They were back in a flash and I lifted the limp body and laid it carefully

I'M MOVING BACK TO MARS

in the bottom of the cage. It was so cute, so tiny, and so helpless. Covering the top with a heavy wooden board, I carried the cage to our enclosed porch and sat it on the bar. "Alright, everyone back to the table. I'll call the power company .... and get your broccoli out from under your napkins."

It was not until the lights came on that we realized that Stubby (that's what we named him during dinner) was missing from his cage. Our screened porch opened into the house and he could be anywhere. "Everyone, man your posts", I barked. We already had a plan formulated from when our seven foot black snake escaped last month. Each child grabbed a bath towel and stood at their pre-assigned post while the little missus took up her position on top of our bed.

I was the reconnaissance guy who would roam the house and flush out Stubby. After locating him under the couch, I called for backup and the kids closed in. You cannot believe how fast a three legged tree rat can run when not wanting to be caught.

For the next half hour the four of us dashed from one piece of furniture to the next, missing every time with our towels. Finally, exhausted from running, Stubby made a wrong turn and we nailed him.

Once I presented a couple of Polaroid pictures of our captive safely back in his cage with a twenty pound cinder block on top, the little missus descended from her perch.

Entering the living room, she shrieked in horror. Our new beige carpet was covered with tiny blood marks from

Stubby's missing leg wound. While I cleaned the carpet, I pondered my decision to help this little varmint.

I think I was on blood dot 217 when my daughter announced, "Dad, promise you won't get mad." With that one statement, the little missus headed for her post on top of the bed. "Stubby was sooooo thirsty, I gave him water but he jumped out instead." I ran to seal off the porch from the house.

"Man your posts again", I angrily growled. The towels were still in the washer, so each of us took a weapon. A yard rake, a broom and the porch squeegee would have to suffice. For the next hour we hunted and found nothing.

"Take a break", I announced and made a few phone calls to several animal shelters. "Excuse me, I hate to bother you at this hour, but we have a three legged tree rat loose in our house and can't find it. Do you think........hello.... hello."

"I am not sleeping in this house. We'll check into a hotel." my wife demanded. "How about the camper"? I knew her silence meant OK. It took me an hour to set up the camper because it was now raining hard, soaking me to the bone. When the rain stopped, I carried bedding into the camper when I spotted something small sitting right in the middle of the back yard.

I trained my flashlight on the object and spotted a small, red, three legged tree rat staring back. It was Stubby and I sensed he was laughing at me. Later that evening, we found a small exit hole chewed in the porch screen.

The next morning I put signs up in the neighborhood. "WARNING: DANGEROUS THREE LEGGED TREE RAT, WEARING DESIGNER OUTFIT, ROAMING THIS AREA. IF SPOTTED, RUN".

F.W., PHONE HOME

I'm getting rid of my phone, plain and simple. No ifs, ands, or buts; it's gone. I am done, finis, it's over. My love affair with phones is history. So if you want to talk to me, swing by the house or send smoke signals because if you call my house you will get a recording that says, "We're sorry but the subscriber has flipped out and has destroyed every phone in his house. Try later after he has taken his lithium."

Outside of my bladder, the telephone has taken over what little control I have left of my life. I've got to get rid of it because it is so domineering, so rude. It always manages to ring at the most inopportune times. No matter what is going on, when that phone rings, it demands that I drop what I'm doing and race to pick it up. Just this month it has managed to interrupt two romantic moments (don't ask), burn one dinner and send me racing through the house soaking wet, looking for where I left it, usually outside. But those are minor compared to three major events that occurred just this week.

First, I must tell you that my wife and I never argue. Instead, we debate. This has worked well for us because, as debaters, we remain more civilized. It's kind of like fencing. The winner makes a kill and you don't realize you've been run through until it's too late. It's so much cleaner than arguing. You're not allowed to throw things or use bad language. Crying is considered hitting below the belt.

Anyway, our last debate was titled, "What dumb, bone-headed bozo lost the checkbook?" This was a sensitive topic for me, since the checkbook is under my care and control. My wife is an excellent debater and usually wins, but on this particular issue, I thought of a great line that would finish her off, causing me to win, hands down.

Then, the dad-ratted phone rang, the debate had to be put on hold for fifteen minutes and later, when the call was finished, I couldn't remember my killer line. As I racked my brain, trying to remember why she was the true bone-head, she finished me off with a verbal "Stocatta" (a thrust to the lower abdomen, where I am very sensitive) and ended the debate with a smirking "Touché." Her final thrust convinced me I was the bone-headed bozo that lost the checkbook.

Why did I lose the debate? The phone, of course. Who lost the checkbook is not the issue. Who won the debate is all that counts. I've got to get rid of the phone. Later, the check book was found, deep in her purse, where I must have placed it mistakenly. Who cares, I lost the debate.

Then, yesterday, I was in the top of my hemlock tree, picking off wooly adelgids and putting them in a tin can when my wife announced I had an important phone call. Climbing down, I accidentally spilled the half full can and the woolly's fell to the ground, racing off into the forest to hide. It would take me hours to round them up. Reaching the ground, I was

I'M MOVING BACK TO MARS

angrier than a tourist looking for a restroom; madder than a local behind a Floridian driving through the gorge. More livid than a..... Well, you got the picture.

Picking up the phone, I listened to the dial tone for over a minute, not believing the person had hung up on me. I just know all the woolly's were out there laughing at me. Later, I would learn that the call was from a pesticide company wanting to inspect my hemlock for wooly's. I don't need a pesticide company to tell me I'm infested. I just spilled a half can of the critters on the ground, who are now high fiving each other over their good fortune. The phone, the phone, got to get rid of the phone.

But the worst of the worst of the worst occurred this morning. This was the deciding moment for me. This was the knockout punch, the end of phonedom at my house, the final straw, the real reason I must get rid of my phone. I was just about to take off my - oops, hold it. Is that the phone? It is the phone ringing. I'll be right back --------------------.

LADIES, DO NOT READ THIS COLUMN

I am writing this article strictly for you guys out there so ladies, read no further. Gentlemen, if you have never been to a Yoga class, get up off your duff and attend one. I went with my wife and was shocked to learn what goes on in those classes. Two things will be revealed immediately. First, you will know just how women everywhere have been able to take over our planet. Secondly, you will find out what you have suspected for years, but always avoided thinking about. Your body is nothing more than a large mass of mush.

To start, you will have to first buy a pair of those disgusting black stretch tights that will reveal every single fat gram you have ever consumed since your birth. Midriff tops are in vogue but I chose the more macho muscle or tank top shirt, even though it revealed my "Gimme Some Lovin'" tattoo.

You will be the only guy there and all the women will look at you with "Why are you here?" looks of disdain, but don't let them run you off for their secret will soon be revealed.

Class starts with soft oriental music, incense and breathing exercises. I found this part easy as I have been breathing for a very long time. Then, the instructor makes you get into really weird positions and stay there while you meditate and hum. This is best accomplished by putting your thumbs and middle fingers together for reasons I have not figured out yet, but it might be a secret signal they use.

Class got harder and harder and then it dawned on me this instructor just might be my first grade teacher, Sister Whazername, returning to finish me off. Next, the lady in front of me, from the sitting position, placed both legs behind her shoulder blades and began to hum and meditate. Can you imagine her husband waking in the middle of the night to find her sitting up in bed in that position? Is that scary or what?

But the best part of the class was when it was revealed to me that while they are all meditating and humming, they are really sending subliminal messages to men everywhere to acquiesce to all female commands. I know this because as class progressed, I felt mentally weakened, being overpowered by

I'M MOVING BACK TO MARS

their thoughts. This is how we have been overthrown. This is why we are left with nothing more then honey-do lists, heavy lifting and the NFL. Yoga is their secret weapon.

After class, the girls and I headed to the Pink Palace Health Bar for refreshments. Yogurt with wheat germ is the favorite but I chose the split pee smoothie. That's when the idea hit me. I will counter these attacks by opening my own yoga spa for men. Ideas raced through my head. Here is how it will work.

The first thing you notice when entering my spa is that there is only a men's room. There, you will find used, dirty hand towels on the floor and draped over the sink, left by other members. They will remain there forever. All the toilet seats are in the upright position, just as they are on Mars.

In the main exercise room, you will find eight layers of egg carton foam padding on the floor for your comfort. Class begins with the soft music of Jimmy Buffet's Margaritaville. I will instruct you get into the sitting position and expel all the bad air from your alveolar lobes. Belching and burping is encouraged to release gasses from your pancake and country ham breakfast. Next, into the prone position, where you will put your arms gently on your stomach. If this is impossible for you, lay them on your chest. Now close your eyes and hum. Clear your mind of all things except taking back control of the planet. Concentrate, meditate, breathe deep, and keep your eyes closed. Now relax every single muscle in your body, especially the jaw muscle. Allow your mouth to fall open gently. Continue to think about taking back the planet by sending subliminal messages to women everywhere. Now continue doing this for the next ten minutes. Are you concentrating? Zzzzzzzzzzzzzzzzz.

HIGHLANDS NEEDS A FEW GALLUS DOMESTICUS CANNONS

I have many sources of information that come into my office on a regular basis. As a big time column writer for an important newspaper, these sources are invaluable in assisting me in getting the really important news out to our readers. That is what I do, the cutting edge, so to speak. The Woodstork and Bernberg of Highlands. Was that their names?

First, I research the material for authenticity and then determine whether it would be interesting to read. Well, I hope you're sitting down and if not, do so right now before you read any further for you are not going to believe what has just crossed my desk.

The United States Government has just completed a series of secret tests on a new weapon which fires dead roosters at airplane windshields. I swear this is the truth.

The rooster cannon, or Gallus Domesticus Gun, is used to test the strength of airplane windshields when hit by flying birds. The contractor for this new weapon is somewhere at a secret plant in Tennessee, which, of course, is the home of where all dead roosters go if their ambition is to wind up splattered across a windshield.

I'M MOVING BACK TO MARS

They feel it would be better to wind up there than on your plate. That is the current thinking of most of the upscale feathered critters that I know. The results of early tests are still under lock and key, but my sources say they can also substitute chickens into this new arsenal, as the guns are gender blind. This is good because, at last count, there were far more chickens out there than roosters. Anyway, it would be improper for the government to show bias, smashing only the male species against the glass.

What does all this have to do with Highlands, you ask? I say, plenty. Just use your imagination. Do you realize what uses these cannons could be for us if we could just get our hands on a few of them?

For example, have you noticed that no one, and I mean no one, is obeying the walk, don't walk lights on Main Street. As a retired law enforcement guy, I always want to obey the law, regardless of how stupid it is, like standing on the corner of 4th and Main Street at 11 PM waiting for the walk light to come on when there is not even one car with its engine running in the entire town. Recently I tried to inform a group of scofflaw pedestrians of their violation and they simply looked at me like I was crazy, which, of course, I am. I got caught in the herd and was carried into the street, not even in the direction I wanted to go.

I think with a little ingenuity, we could rig the Gallus Domesticus cannons to motion sensors at each intersection which could fire dead chickens at violators crossing against the light. I know this might seem a might harsh, so I would recommend we downsize the rooster cannons to Cornish hen size, making less of an impact as it hits the violator in the chest. Chickadees would be the perfect size, except I would have the Audubon Society all over me. In any case these wrong-doers would soon get the message and, as an added incentive to never violate the signal again, they would get to keep the hen.

Now hold it, I know organizations like the A.C.L.U. will scream "foul" on this one and claim we are violating someone's rights. I say chicken fodder. Even if they are right, Highlands is involved in so many pending law suits now that one more won't make any difference. The U.S. Supreme Court has not had a good chicken case in years and Highlands could become even more famous if we could, just once, win one. This could be our big moment in history.

NEVER SAY "Hmmm"

Here is how it all happened. Whenever the little missus has an issue to discuss with me and she knows I will disagree or be uncomfortable with the topic, she does it when I am in deep REM sleep. She feels this is the best time for calmness when discussing difficult matters because she knows I will say "Hmmm" to any question asked while I'm in this comatose state. To her "Hmmm" means yes. To me, "Hmmm" means "Don't talk to me while I'm sleeping." It would not be nice for me to say she took advantage of me, so instead, let me just say, "Darn-tooten she took advantage of me."

She employed this system on me last year and I woke up to

I'M MOVING BACK TO MARS

find I had agreed to visit her Aunt, Beatrice McAfee, in west Poughkeepsie. (I lovingly refer to her as BM.) I don't like going there because she spits little pieces of food at me when she talks. It's especially gross when she eats spinach. Did I mention that REM stands for "Reprogramming Every Man?"

Last month, I woke from a wonderful night's sleep to learn I had agreed to move. No, not just from Florida to Highlands for the summer. Ha, I can do that with one leg tied behind my back if the car is automatic. I mean move, as in taking every single thing I own and put it someplace else. I have only moved three times in my entire adult life and the first time I had so little stuff it fit in the trunk of my "55" Olds. This time it was scary. Remember, women are gatherers of stuff.

We set up an elaborate moving and control system. All boxes with numbers on them belonged to her and had accompanying three by five index cards, listing all the items contained in the box. Each room was color coded and boxes corresponded with those assigned colors. Of course, each box was sanitized prior to packing and tightly sealed when full.

Boxes without numbers were mine and could contain anything from used motor oil to dress shirts. This explains why there is a chain saw and greasy rag still sitting on our dresser. As a man, I choose the simpler system.

Yes, there was some stress, but the little missus and I gave up fighting way back. Instead, we "debate." During our big move, we had so many wonderful debates and, even though I did loose a sizeable amount of them, it was fun to be in the contest. Debate choke marks on our necks have almost disappeared.

Our most recent debate was over me asking a very stupid question, like "Why would anyone want to own 2,342 extra plastic coat hangers." She won that debate, hands down, with the perfect answer, "They were on sale."

The best part about making the big move is that you get to see stuff you haven't visited since your last move. "That belonged to my mother" is the catchall phrase we use to mean we would store it away until our next move. Of course, when we finally croak, our kids will throw it all out, including the sun-suit I wore when I was 11 months old. If you are interested in seeing this awesome sun-suit, see me before I die.

The most exciting part of our adventure was when we came across our very old.... no, very, very old picture albums of when we were kids. Exciting, not because of having the pleasure of looking through the memorabilia because we never got that far. Exciting because of our confrontation with a strange looking yellow and grey stuff that was growing, pulsating and glowing on the outside of the albums. I once saw this stuff in a ***Star Trek*** episode and it took over the whole ship. Fearing the worse, we quickly resealed the box and will let our children deal with it.

Eventually we got into our new digs and life returned to normal; well, normal for us. By the time the last picture was hung and everything was in its place, it was time to re-pack for Highlands.

We are currently numbering and color coding boxes. Mine are the ones with a big "H" on the box which does not stand for Highlands, it stands for Hmmm.

THE RITE OF MAKING MY WRONG RIGHT

Unbeknownst to anyone, I have been taking private writing lessons from a secret tutor who has been helping me be more better in my language construction when I write articles for this newspaper that is free and comes out once a week and can be found in all the little green cans that are scattered around Highlands in many places and other places not in the little green cans like the Highlands Recreation Park and Mountain Fresh Grocery and many other places not in the little green cans in over 100 places and I have been getting better in my writing but have had to recently fire my writing tutor for her continuous hounding me about my run-on sentences and I just couldn't take it anymore.

That is not the only reason that I fired her. She was also nagging me for using the "that" word too much and for that, I sent her packing so that I don't have to hear about that anymore. She is gone and that's that.

I have been doing this "writing thing" for a long time. Back in my other life as a police officer, report writing is what I did about half my life. Policemen are required to write about everything they do and see. After you have been writing police reports for awhile, you learn to become more creative so you can protect yourself from criticism. This, of course, is called CYA.

Although you were not allowed to begin arrest reports with "Once upon a time," the more creative your reports were, the better you looked. There are many ways to tell the same story, so why not tell it in a way that makes you look good? This was the beginning of my creative writing exercises known as W.E.L.P, the "Wooldridge Embellishment Language Process."

Then there was this other little gizmo called the "incident" report. If you found yourself in a situation where none of the 321 different kinds of police reports fit, you would fill out an incident report. We even had a "no report" report you would fill out to explain why you didn't feel it was necessary to write a report. Could I make this up?

Each day, a large police department generates a ton of paperwork which is all turned into a dark, scary little place called "report review," where little cone headed people check your writing for accuracy. These editors of police never saw daylight and were pasty skinned grammar experts who would reject your report if needed. I always had good relations with these people because I would slide food under their door with my name on it.

Once I left the department, I went into writer's withdrawal. I woke up on a Monday morning retired and found I suddenly had nothing to report on or write down. I panicked.

Fortunately, I was going into the rappelling business and would have to deal with the United States Forest Service who kept me writing stuff down for the next thirteen years. There was no need to go cold turkey, thanks to them.

I'M MOVING BACK TO MARS

But time marches on and finally I got too old to dangle from cliffs all day, so I retired again. I was OK for awhile because the Forest Service required me to write reports on why I didn't want to hang from their cliffs anymore.

Since God always looks out for drunks, small children and satire writers, I had just finished my last Forest Service report when I got picked up by a local newspaper to continue my embellishments of life in a weekly column.

Life was great. For the first time, I could write outrageous stuff, offend everyone and make people who I didn't offend that particular week, laugh at what I wrote. Then, fate had its way with me, because I dropped by the news office one morning and found that during the night, corporate leaders had swooped in and replaced everyone. I was toast.

This time I did panic. I called my police department to see if they had anything they wanted me to write. "Fred who?" was their reply. Even the Forest Service rejected me, calling me repelling.

Then, just as I was going into major withdrawal by sitting in the corner of my closet and rocking back and forth, I got a call from my current editor. Even better, she is not a cone-head and does not have pasty skin. I am concerned because she keeps rejecting the food I slide under her door.

FRED WOOLDRIDGE

WHEN I GROW UP, I'M GOING TO BE A FLAG MAN

The guy sitting patiently in his Mercedes spent eight years in med school, two more years interning, two years of working E. R. and finally he is allowed to practice medicine. The guy right behind him spent six hard years of study at law school, starved to death as a prosecutor for two years and is now with a law firm and doing just OK. The lady behind the doctor and the lawyer is a care giver for a cancer patient who is waiting to die at home. And I could go on and on.

What do all these people have in common? Their lives are on hold and controlled by the flag man who learned his trade in two hours. The doctor will be late for surgery, the lawyer will be in big time trouble with the judge for missing the hearing and the cancer patient will become more depressed because she needs a hug from her care giver. They are all sitting on the highway until the flag man says they can go. If he's in a bad mood, that could take awhile.

When I grow up (ha), I definitely will be a flag man. What a power trip this will be for me. With a mere flip of the wrist, I can hold up traffic forever, if I want. Maybe you will go; maybe not. Depends on how I feel. If I see a person all dressed up, like wearing a tie, he is toast. Even our president has to wait his turn to have the privilege to ride past me. I have visions of being the best flag man that ever brought progress to a halt. I will turn mediocrity into an art form.

When I do graduate from flag man school, I plan on ignoring the rescue vehicle with his lights flashing and siren

I'M MOVING BACK TO MARS

blaring 30 cars back. I will be known as the "Mad Dog" flag guy of the world. Wow, what control I will have over everyone's lives.

Becoming a flag man is not easy. Flag man school is tough. Actually there is no flag involved, unless you are one of those uppity flag men from a construction site.

Regular flag men must be able to hold a pole with the words "slow" on one side and "stop" on the other. You must be able to distinguish between the two and operate this pole efficiently while holding a walkie talkie radio in the other hand. This requires an I.Q. of 100 or better. That would be 50 for each of the two flag men involved.

The walkie talkie is a vital part of the flag man operation. When he spots a hot babe with her skirt pulled just a little higher than normal, he can radio the whole construction crew of the approaching "sag." The reason highway projects take so long to complete is because of "sagging," which means the gawking at female motorists as they pass. A good "sag" of a really hot babe can stop work for over an hour; ten seconds to actually observe the chick as she rolls by and 59 minutes and 50 seconds to talk about her after she's gone. Construction crew members bid for sagging positions. The higher up, the better the sag.

When I am flag man, all those people who shout nasty things at me as they finally pass will pay later. On their next trip, they will sit and wait for at least thirty minutes and when they finally do pass, I will give them a smile and friendly wave. You don't get to be a "Mad Dog" flag man by being nice.

To actually get the feel of what it's going to be like to be a flag man, I went out into the field and actually got an interview with a veteran flag man. His name is Dilbert, of course.

Here are segments of our conversation: "Hello, Dilbert, tell our readers what your life is like as a flag man." (Long pause) "You know what's good? Pearl beer and popcorn. Ever tried that? Hold on, Mr. Newspaper man, while I gaze upon this little country club chippy pulling up here. I think she winked at me yesterday. Hold on a sec. while I alert the boys so they can get into position".

Hmmm, maybe I won't have to wait to grow up to be a flag man.

I LOVE DEER HUNTERS

I am going on the record here. Hello, are you reading this? I love deer hunters. I have close friends who are deer hunters. I have eaten venison and like it. I own a deer rifle and like to sip "Jack." I know all the latest hunting jokes (mostly bad) and love to sit around camp fires at night, spitting and scratching my groin. I will do everything I have to do to earn the respect of my deer hunter buddies short of shooting a defenseless deer. I'm hopeless, what else can I say?

I even hired an instructor (you must remember Dilbert) but he gave up on me because of my ineptness at hunting critters. I'm a true city slicker.... 100%. God once said, "Let there be Fred, let him dwell in the city in the winter and in Highlands in the summer. Let him hunt humans." POW; I did.

I'M MOVING BACK TO MARS

While I completely and totally understand the philosophy behind "the hunt" and the thinning out the herd theory, I cannot overcome my love of deer, live ones. They hold a special place in my heart.

While traveling through a state park on the California coast, the little missus and I stopped our car to study a map. We were startled by a small herd of deer that approached the open windows of our car, obviously looking for a handout. For the next twenty minutes, we just stared at each other, all of us motionless. They are such beautiful creatures.

So when I get to be President (I gave up on being a flag man 'cause there's just too much responsibility) I will change the law on hunting and killing deer. Here is how it will work.

Deer hunting season will be open twelve months a year. Any person, who wishes to kill deer and can prove he is living below the national poverty level, can purchase a permit to kill as many deer as it takes to feed the hunter's family. That solves the thinning out problem and puts venison on poor people's table all year long.

No one else will need a permit or license to hunt deer all year. They just can't kill them. Enter the camera rifle, a specially designed rifle which takes high speed pictures of whatever is in the cross-hairs. It feels and looks like a rifle, fires a blank cartridge, kicks like a rifle and startles the deer when you pull the trigger. The only difference is the deer lives and you wind up with a 10 x 12 photo of your kill in awesome color, complete with cross hairs in the picture. Of course, if you miss the deer, you throw the picture away.

I ran the idea by Dilbert and he looked at me as if someone had just pooped on his ham sandwich. Then I realized Dilbert just looks poor but makes six figures a year doing bulldozer work. He wouldn't even be able to mooch venison from his poor friends because he doesn't have any. Sorry, Dilbert, you'll just have to stick with those savory steaks you got squirreled away in your freezer.

Years ago I knew a man who loved deer even more than me. During the off season, he fed the deer and slowly moved their food into his open barn. The deer began to hang around the barn and slept there at night. By the time hunting season started, he had over a dozen deer frequenting the open barn.

The evening before hunting season, he would close the barn door and trap the deer inside. He fed them and gave them water throughout the season, releasing them the day after the season closed. This, of course, is against the law and he came within a cat's whisker of going to jail when someone tipped off officials. The deer were released and slaughtered within the week.

Since I probably won't be president before the first day of deer season, thousands of hunters will be up before dawn and sitting in their tree stands so they can be the first to nail a deer. When Dilbert took me out hunting, I saw so many hunters on opening day, I suggested that maybe the Government needed to thin out the herd. This went over like a motorcycle rally at the Chamber's Music Festival annual gala so I dropped the subject. It's probably one of the reasons I am currently banned from the woods during hunting season. In the near future, I will open a school to teach deer to look up.

I'M DECOMPOSING

I ain't even dead yet

This should not be happening. Body decomposition is not supposed to occur until way after the backhoe has finished tamping dirt on top of your new home. But it is happening. I am decomposing and I am still breathing.

How could this be happening, you ask? It all started a long, long time ago in a scary place called Miami. I used to live there and was a sun worshiper. I lived on the sandy beaches and when I went to work at my first job with Florida Power and Light, I spent the day bare chested and in shorts. Being brown was really the in thing and I was as tan as a white person could get. That is until I met the little missus.

Because my entire life was spent out on the beach, it should be no surprise that I met her waist deep in the Atlantic Ocean. I will not tell you what year that was in fear she will speed up my decomposition, but this pretty, petite dark haired girl was tanner than I. POW, there was instant attraction and it was only moments later we were comparing skin tone by holding our arms next to each other. How romantic. Now I had someone to bake my body with and the two of us spent endless hours lying prone in the sun. Friendship turned to love and the rest is history.

FRED WOOLDRIDGE

Flash ahead a zillion years to 1999. While rappelling, I slammed my thumb against a granite rock and in a matter of hours it was sore and purple. In time it healed but not perfect. The nail was deformed (stay with me `cause it gets better... ah, worse) and for the next two years I just put up with occasional soreness and deformity. Then I read an article that said I may have nail rot which may be incurable without prescription medication.

I panicked because I am terrified of doctors. They always want to shove something up my rectum. No matter what you go in for, sooner or later, they will want to do that. I was relieved to learn I would have to see a dermatologist as they are not known for wanting to invade you.

Once in the office, I displayed my deformed nail to the doctor. "This is not a biggie," I confidently announced as he walked into my cubicle. Ignoring my nail, he immediately stared at my arms. "Take off your shirt and lie down on your stomach." My eyes widened. This is a perfect example of why you should never go to the doctor unless your whole arm has been ripped from your shoulder. As I ran for the door he assured me this did not involve an invasion of my privacy, at least not below my waist line.

After a quick examination, he called in a colleague and an intern to take a gander at my back. Now I have three pair of hands (a cheap thrill for me) probing me while they engaged in doctor talk. I did pick up on a few words like "and," "but" and "hmmm." I am really getting nervous.

"What about my thumb nail" I asked? He ignored my question and says, "I would like to take a few samples of tissue decomposition from your back. It is painless and, although you have hundreds, I only want four or five." "Yikes, my back is decomposing" I asked? "Relax, it's a good thing. I see you spend a great deal of time in the sun and that you are fair skinned. There are a small number of white, fair skinned people in the world who never get skin cancer and we don't know why. Instead of cancer, they get small blemishes of decomposed tissue. They are harmless and we could really use them for our research."

I was still not convinced he would, sooner or later, break out the chrome choo-choo train and want to violate my dignity, but I agreed to the surgery. Elated, they went right to work. The process was painless and a half hour later I left his office with four Band-aids on my back and a deformed thumb nail.

Oh yes, the thumb nail. The doctor did give me a prescription for a medicated nail polish I had to apply for the next eight weeks. I thank God it did not come in pink.

THE DANGLING CHAD

Blame the turtles

No, no, no, the "Dangling Chad" is not a gay bar in Palm Beach. I'm talking about that little piece of cardboard (a chad) left hanging from a voting card in Palm Beach County that set this nation on its heels in 2000. Surely you remember those bug eyed guys with magnifying glasses staring at voting cards? The whole nation was focused on Palm Beach.

More shocking than the upheaval over the chad was the realization that this entire nation was under the complete control of the turtles. George Bush wound up winning by 537 votes and carried Florida. Ironically, the turtles put him in the White House. It was the turtles who were so duh they cast thousands of votes for Pat Buchanan when they meant to vote for Al Gore. (Is that funny...ah, maybe not?) It was the turtles who started the ruckus because they did not have the strength to completely punch out the chad and here's the best part. Ninety percent of all turtles are Democrats who still have their shorts in a wad over what happened.

In order to be a Palm Beach turtle, you must first be at least 70 years of age and have shrunk in height to five feet or less. You also must live in a condo, wear sneakers, play bingo on Wednesday afternoon and drive a 300 hp, 27 foot long Cadillac or Lincoln. This, of course, is how they became turtles, with their little heads barely sticking up above the side windows.

Florida has been working hard at correcting the voting problem and the brain trusts have come up with electronic touch screen monitors with no paper trail as the answer. This was a good idea because turtles were born before TV and the most sophisticated piece of electronics they have ever operated is an electric mixer.

I'M MOVING BACK TO MARS

Let's fantasize for a moment. The turtle enters the polling booth, closes the curtain and stares at a monitor covered with dirty finger marks. The curtain flies open and the turtle complains there is no remote control clicker in the booth. A tired, not so polite, attendant explains to the turtle that you merely touch the picture of the person you want to be the next president of the United States. The monitor will record your selection and ask you if you are sure. If you are, touch the big "yes" on the screen. Pow, you just voted.

The turtle reenters the booth. Seconds later the curtain flies open again and the turtle complains "John Kerry's picture is not on this screen." The attendant enters the booth with the turtle and points to Kerry's picture, careful not to touch the screen. "That's not Kerry, that's Pat Buchanan," the turtle complains. "Kerry's face is longer." The attendant reaches over and adjusts the vertical knob, making Kerry's face even longer than it is. "That's still not Kerry. He is handsome and this man is ugly. I think this one is Kerry." The turtle reaches over and touches the picture of George Bush. The attendant announces, "You just voted for Bush. Is that who you want to be president?" "You guys tricked us four years ago with that Buchanan switch and you're not going to get away with it again." Smirking at the attendant, the turtle indignantly smacks the "Yes" block.

One could easily come to the conclusion there is no way to get the vote straight in Palm Beach. More tests are needed. One solution was to have two punching bags with pictures of Bush and Kerry on them with instructions to slug the candidate they dislike. A swing at Bush cast an automatic vote for Kerry. But early tests showed that turtles are not fighters, they're bingo players. If they can't get the chad out of the card, how will they hit the bag?

Enter the bingo card voting system. Hundreds of turtles arrive at the voting place and are given a single voter card. The card has an array of pictures of different people and Bush and Kerry are hidden on the card. The announcer begins to call out numbers, "Under the B -7." If the voter wants the person whose picture appears under B-7 to be president, the turtle calls out "Bingo."

Early test results are promising. Out of the 100 turtles in the test, 27 voted for Bush, 41 for Kerry, 17 for Rabbi Webberman, 9 for Tony, the butcher, 2 for Liberace and 5 for Ralph Nader.

I know, I know, that's 101 votes. Someone voted twice. `Whadaya expect? It's Palm Beach.

"I'LL SHOW YOU MINE, THEN YOU SHOW ME YOURS"

I had just finished converting a giant refrigerator box into a nifty fort, complete with peep holes, a secret entrance and small windows for shooting at the enemy. Then Betty arrived, the girl from down the street and although she didn't have a rifle, I let her come in. After all, she was a third grader and bigger than me.

I decided to assign her the task of "enemy spotter" and was in the middle of explaining her duties when she announced, "I'll show you mine, then you show me yours." Before I could fully understand what that meant, POW, she dropped her drawers. I dropped my rifle and, in a state of shock, pinned myself against the back wall of my fort and stared. My first thoughts were, "No wonder they're all so mean, they're missing important body parts."

I was able to escape unharmed, but to this day, I have been affected by that incident. I think it is the reason I am always so politically incorrect. I must still be mad at Betty for freaking me out. There must still be scars.

I grew up in a world totally run by males with full body parts. The powers at that time would never have relegated authority to people who were without them. In my era, there were mailmen, policemen, firemen and yes, flag men. Women in combat? Get a grip. Women were waitresses, stewardesses, secretaries and stuff like that. They brought coffee to their bosses and jobs befitting people who were missing body parts.

When the world began to change and I didn't, I slowly became more and more politically incorrect. I was a cop during an era when police departments struggled to hire blacks because they constantly flunked the swimming exam. The solution, of course, was to eliminate swimming from the exam. Politically incorrect dummies like me suggested we teach blacks to swim. (Ha)

Then along came police women. I had a real problem with woman cops but had to adjust to survive. By the time I retired, the department was hiring tiny munchkin types who could have auditioned for the remake of The Wizard of Oz. I wonder what London, England thinks of us?

I am also down on fat cops. In my era, the department made sure you were in top physical condition to get hired, then allowed you to turn into a fat slob once training was over. I got in lots of trouble over my politically incorrect conduct on that issue. Today, police officers just get hired fat. Retirement is good.

In a fight over physical training for police officers, the "Miami Herald" newspaper featured an article titled (I am not making this up) "The Fat Wimps Won" after I lost a duel with the police union over physical training for officers. Am I politically incorrect, or what?

During my tenure, one of my fellow officers was a cross dressing, homosexual who took off his clothes in a gay strip joint after he got off duty. Could I make this up? I was so politically incorrect, I disapproved but didn't know what to call him, so I just stuck with "unprofessional."

So I guess I will always be politically incorrect and it's getting worse, thanks to Betty.

I believe women should not play in the NFL or be in combat. They should not be towel valets in men's rooms nor should they be lifting cargo on the loading docks at seaports.

Because I still view them as the weaker sex, politically incorrect dummies like me still hold the door for women, even strangers. I still say "Yes Ma'am" to women who are older than me (there are a few) and come to their rescue if they are in trouble. I once raced over to help a lady who was struggling to get a large box into the trunk of her car. She screamed and ran from me because she thought I was going to mug her. I truly need to move back to Mars.

I believe we should have empathy for people who are missing body parts. They should receive extra care and attention. Until the arrival of policewomen, I would never have used foul language in front of a woman. They taught me how to do that and a lot more.

Yes, I still blame Betty for flashing me at I time when I was so impressionable and vulnerable. I never did show her "mine." She wouldn't have been impressed anyway.

MEET MISTER GRUMP

(I am anti Santa)

Am I grumpy or what? Digging through my desk drawer, I can't find the credit card I know I tossed in there a year ago. The one in my wallet is maxed out and I still have lots of buying to do.

There are long lines at every store. I am putting gas in the car every other day and the prices are outrageous. I never get headaches, but now I have one. Traffic is horrendous and the store parking lots are full. Jockeying for a spot takes fortitude and courage. Ho, Ho, Ho, are we having fun yet?

It is the Christmas shopping season and I am wondering why I did this to myself. Back in August, in a moment of sheer weakness, I told the little missus I would help her Christmas shop. She didn't forget. Women never forget. Even though I know women are "gatherers" and men are "hunters". I still said yes, forgetting momentarily that we have a large family, all hungry for presents under the tree.

In past years she did all the Christmas shopping and I decorated the front of the house. We did the tree and interior of the house together. This plan has worked well. What was I thinking? Am I jolly and bright? Nah!

We have just spent two hours looking for a battery operated CD player for my granddaughter. This common item can be found in every store imaginable but we are looking in the fourth store, with two more to go. Why? The player has to be pink.

Why do I have this strange feeling that my granddaughter knew this when she included it on her list? Maybe she is getting even with us for making her sit through a lengthy ballet. Finally, out of desperation, the little missus announced, "I'll buy this blue one and take it back once I spot a pink one." I was going to ask, "Then why buy the blue one?" but decided I didn't want to know. (Remember, they are from another planet.) She made the purchase and, BAM, one down, seventy six to go.

This is how it has been the past two weeks. Furthermore, I am up to here (a gesture here, possibly obscene.) with Santa Clauses. There are hundreds of them, most with their hands out, collecting for who knows what. Yesterday I got my windshield washed by a Santa who was collecting pocket change for booze. Now my windshield is dirtier than before. Merry Christmas, sucker.

When we left J.C. Penney we found our car had a flat tire. I had run over a bolt that could have held the San Francisco bridge together. The tire was ruined. $148.00 and two and half hours later, we are headed for our next adventure, the Toys "R" Us store.

We are looking for the Chou Chou doll. Not just any Chou Chou doll, but the one on sale that comes with diaper bag, diapers, artificial poop and a complete change of clothes. Like all babies, this little gal runs up your credit card bill because, even on sale, she costs $29.95. How much is artificial poop, anyway?

There are 187 varieties of dolls in this store and with all the hired help busy, we spent over an hour looking for the right Chou Chou only to find we had the wrong Chou Chou when it was finally our turn at a long check out line. Headed back into the doll section we did stop in the Builder Bob's area for a fast lunch of peanut butter crackers and apple. Fa la la la la, la la la la.

At the end of the day we had 6 purchases. On the way home, while sitting in stalled traffic from an accident up ahead, I suggested it would be good to buy gift cards for the remainder of the family. I could do it on line while sipping cool eggnog with cinnamon. Each family member could go to the store and buy whatever they wanted. This suggestion did not go over big with the little missus and she mumbled something under breath about me being from Mars.

So this year, my Christmas season has taken on new meaning. Shop till you drop, then shop some more. Once that's completed, we shop for food, lots of food. Then we wrap presents in between house cleaning and getting the decorations out of the attic. Buy the tree. Was it that lopsided when we picked it out? Decorate the front of the house, then the inside.

Is it any wonder we sometimes forget the true meaning of Christmas? Who has time for the birth of Christ with all this shopping and work to get done? Wouldn't it be great if we could chuck it all and concentrate on the real meaning of this celebration? Nah......... the economy would collapse.

ALL MY REAL ENEMIES ARE FINALLY DEAD

A pompous report

Eddie Crawley, my fifth grade enemy, thought his mission in life was to make me miserable. Finally, near the end of the school year, Eddie and I had it out in the school playground. It was worth the five day detention and ruler across my knuckles, just to be able to get my licks in. We graduated from St. Bridget's School, still enemies. I have lost track of him over the years but, if he is alive, he's my only enemy.

In my other life as a flat foot, I had scary enemies who wanted me dead. Just ask around. After my retirement, I had to keep track of the really serious ones and I am happy to report they are all dead. Most were murdered by their own enemies, two killed in prison, but some died of old age. The departmental joke, when I retired in 1989, was if I turned up murdered, the homicide unit wouldn't know where to begin. Funny, but not so funny.

I acquired most of my really serious enemies during my years with the Strategic Investigations Unit. (SIU) That's a fancy word which means I was making enemies faster than Saddam Hussein. My job was to make organized hoodlums miserable and I worked hard at it. My success was measured by the number of bad guys who hated me. Most active cops learn to ignore prison talk and street rumors about criminals getting even, but in 1977, I was called to the chief's office and told by two FBI agents that a guy I'll just call Peanuts, had ordered a contract for my death. I used to haunt the guy endlessly.

Like most hoodlums, Peanuts was an active organized crime figure busy with the usual, ho hum bookmaking, narcotics, untaxed cigarettes and booze, etc. This guy would actually wake up his two young sons in the middle of the night and send them out on their bikes to see if they could spot us on surveillance. Eventually, someone slit the kids' bike tires and the practice ended. Peanuts was desperate. He even had his doctor call me to ask if I would leave him alone for awhile because of his high blood pressure. That was a bad mistake.

Fortunately the guy Peanuts hired to snuff me was dating a girl who was a DEA informant. In those days, the DEA and the FBI actually talked to one another, if you can believe that, and we were tipped. Active hits on police officers are rare and easily handled by phone. The underworld is notified by law enforcement officials that we know about the hit and if harm comes to anyone, there will be hell to pay. Peanuts got the right call from New York and the hit was cancelled. Not too exciting, but that's how it works.

Just to be cautious, everyone felt it would be good if I would disappear for awhile. I packed my family, pulled my kids out of school and headed for Highlands. When the little missus asked what is going on, I told her I just needed to cool off from work for awhile. She never asked for particulars. That's what a good cop's wife does.

After retirement and opening a rappel business in Highlands, there were less than a half dozen guys left for me to be concerned about. The worse of my living enemies was a young, nasty character named Tony Benvenesti. Once, while serving a search warrant, he shoved an automatic weapon right into my stomach and pulled the trigger. The gun failed to fire because of a defective firing pin. I got to live and he went away for twenty years. He vowed to get me, was eventually released from prison on good behavior and disappeared, which made me real jittery. A year later, his badly decomposed body was found in the Hudson river. Life is good.

The US Forest Service would have been furious with me if they had known I went to work each day with an arsenal close at hand. They certainly weren't going to protect me and I just couldn't chance it. Only my co-workers knew. Retired cops are always vulnerable because they lose their cloak of protection.

Early one morning, while rigging a site for the day's work, a man appeared out of nowhere at the top of the cliff. When I caught sight of him from the corner of my eye, I was startled and turned to face him. My back pack, carrying my weapon, was several feet away. I would never get to it in time. My heart was pounding. "Morning," I said as I walked slowly toward the pack. The man smiled. "I have been watching you rig. What you do is interesting. Well, have a nice day and be careful." He turned and disappeared into the forest. I called out. "Your name's not Eddie Crawley, is it?"

WHY GOD INVENTED DEATH

In the early fifties, my Grandpa told my Ma, "You'll never catch me in one of those airplanes. If God wanted us to fly, we would have been born with wings. Planes are long coffins looking for a place to get buried. Stay far away from them.... and doctors, too, 'cause they're both deadly." Grandpa always seemed to be grumpy about something and I just couldn't understand why. Then I began to age.

I am not sure when I realized that in order to avoid being like my now dead relatives, I would have to work hard at not letting the world run off and leave me. Oh, I fly all the time, but that's not the issue. Resistance to change is the enemy that will eventually make me just like my Grandpa. The same will probably happen to you. Here's why.

You're born knowing nothing. As you grow, you learn

about the world and, at first, are required to accept it just as it is. As you continue to grow, things creep into your world you don't like. You have choices. Resist and try to change it or learn to live with it. That's where the problem starts. Right there, with choices.

Since I learned a long time ago not to spend too much time on things I have no control over, I have been able to adjust quite nicely to world changes so far. But I feel I am slowly losing ground. Even though I have to accept things as they are, I don't have to like them. It is the "not liking" part that is making me just like Grandpa.

For instance, I spent the entire month of December resisting the term "Happy Holiday." I hate Happy Holiday. This is something I can control, at least for myself. I want to say Merry Christmas and, dad-rat-it, I'm going to say Merry Christmas. And when I visit with my Jewish friends, I am going to say Happy Hanukkah. On New Year's day, I'm going to greet everyone with Happy New Year, not Happy Holiday, and I don't care whose calendar it offends. Now, I ask you, is that stage one of getting just like Grandpa, or what?

And while I'm on the holiday thing, I'll tell you I am incensed over the church vs. state issues currently being bantered about. Children can't sing "The Little Drummer Boy" on public property because someone might get offended? Well, I'm offended they can't do that. Are we getting wacky or what? But if I listen to myself rant over this, I sound just like my Grandpa, only the issues are different. I know it's late February, but these things still irk me because I'm getting grumpy, just like Grandpa.

I don't like people who ask me "Are you for or against the war?" I say anyone who says they are for war, has never been in one, like me. Asking that question puts me on the spot. If I say I'm against the war simply because I hate war of any kind, then I could be labeled unpatriotic, which I am not. My Grandpa was in the trenches during World War I and he also hated war. I am sure if I live another ten years, I will be ranting and raving about the evils of war, just like my grandpa.

So if I'm lucky enough to get really old.......I mean old, old, I will probably be totally out of tune with this fast paced world. I will be grumpy because I disagree with everything going on around me. No matter how hard I try, I am not keeping pace with the current thinking on a multitude of issues.

Enter God's gift of death, the great equalizer. The place we are all headed because none of us are going to get out of this alive. A place where the world that passed us by doesn't exist anymore. A place with no airplanes or wars or aggravation about current events. A place of peace. God knew what he was doing in creating death. Doesn't he always?

So the next time you meet a grumpy, old person, try to remember their world may have changed so fast they feel alienated from it. It must be terrible to feel like a foreigner on your own planet.

FRED WOOLDRIDGE

VALENTINE'S DAY
BAH, HUMBUG

I know, I know, you think I'm getting old and grumpy. Well maybe, but I didn't like Valentine's Day even before I was old and grumpy, even way back in the third grade. I only got cards from the ugliest girls in my class and the "hotties" sent me dirty looks when they opened my card that definitely had a life damaging effect on my ego.

This was the same year my parents made me take saxophone lessons because they thought I may have a shot at being president some day. I stood outside Carol Meek's house (now there was a "hottie") on Valentine's Day and played "Cruising Down The River" which was the only song I knew. I was the only kid in my school to be arrested on Valentine's Day for disturbing the peace. So excuse me if I say "BAH, HUMBUG."

Besides, this whole celebration was cooked up by Hallmark to make money - I'm convinced of it. Back in the third grade, cards were only a penny a piece, but now you can buy a card that plays music and sprays rose scent into your nostrils for about four bucks.

To top it all off, this event is religious by nature and offends pagans. Because it is a Christian event, it also offends, Jews, Hindus, Buddhists and Islamic fundamental radicals who want to kill us. It stems from an ancient incident where a Catholic priest named Valentine got his head cut off on February 14th for performing marriages of Roman soldiers. Why do we celebrate people getting their heads cut off? Is this Iraq?

I'M MOVING BACK TO MARS

In 1969, the Catholic Church wisely dropped the practice of honoring St. Valentine for losing his head because no one is sure what really happened. I wish they had done it before I got in the third grade, then I wouldn't have a rap sheet.

For you pagans out there, the roots of Valentine's Day lie in the ancient Roman festival of Lupercalia, which sounds like a skin disease. For 800 years the Romans had dedicated this day to the god Lupercus. On Lupercalia, a young man would draw the name of a young woman in a lottery, and then would keep the woman as a sexual companion for one year. Today we call this "marriage."

After 800 years of this wild, fornicating conduct, Pope Gelasius, pronounced "jealous," condemned the practice and spoiled everyone's fun by changing the lottery to something more mundane which, of course, is anything where sex is not involved.

Oh, I almost forgot about this little tidbit of information. Most birds choose their mates in February, giving added support to my belief that Valentine's Day is "for the birds."

So there you have it. This Valentine's Day celebration is not cracked up to be what you thought and I haven't even mentioned the flowers and candy thing yet. How did all that get started, you ask? It was the brainchild of Whitman Samplers Inc. and F.T.D. of course. Let's see. $4 for the card, $60 for roses, $12 for candy and then there's dinner to the tune of $60 or more, depending on the wine you choose. I'm telling you, this is a right wing conspiracy.

Fortunately, I am married to the little missus, who doesn't

see much value in celebrating this funky event of cutting off Valentine's head. For her, a box of Whitman's candy translates into an extra half inch on the waist. The roses will be dead in several days and the money could be spent on something much more fun. A simple, personalized "I Love You" computer generated card will suffice and dinner will be celebrated on the floor around the coffee table with Schwartzenheimer's bagels and tuna salad while watching reruns of "Friends." Sound boring? Not for us.

Now if I could only persuade her to not make me drag out the sax. and play "Cruising Down The River" in front of the house.

STRANGE PLACES I HAVE STUCK MY TONGUE

Do not try this at home

The first time I ever did this, I was in the fifth grade, just sitting around eating lunch with my buddies in the school cafeteria. One of my friends suggested we all go out to the front of the school and stick our tongues on the school flagpole. At the time, this seemed like a good thing to do, especially in the dead of winter when we're all bored with school and homework.

"Ready? One, two, three, go." Five tongues were pressed tightly against the frozen pole. Instantly, the moisture on our tongues froze, cementing us to the pole. "Ah.... th is lilly un." And so it came to pass that on that bitter cold

I'M MOVING BACK TO MARS

day in Louisville, Ky. I would initiate a new hobby called "tonguing." We originally formed a "tongue" club but, one by one, my buddies dropped out until I was the only one left. Not me. I kept a journal of the places my tongue had been. It was fun to hunt for new and exciting places for me to stick my tongue.

When my parents took me to Washington, D.C., I got to stick my tongue to the brass handles on the Supreme Court doors. I was doing fine until someone opened the door from the inside. But I was fast on my feet and got out of that one without injury. How many people do you know who have done that?

Later on, when I became a teenager, I was not so lucky. I stuck my tongue to the frozen window of my girlfriend's car during an argument and she rolled the window down, taking off several layers of skin as my tongue went inside the car door. I know she did it on purpose.

"Tonguing" got even riskier. My buddy and I had a plan. I would stick my tongue to his frozen tailpipe on his truck and he would start his engine. We would time the event and see how long it took to thaw out and release my tongue from the pipe. Who knew from carbon monoxide? He goofed up though and started the truck in gear and away it went. I lost several layers of tongue skin on that one also.

Then someone said to me, "You're not responsible for where you're born, but you are responsible for where you live." Without any thought to my hobby, I left freezing Louisville for South Florida. While I enjoyed the warm weather, I missed my hobby and longed to stick my tongue on something frozen and unusual. To avoid TTW, (tongue touching withdrawal) I stuck my tongue to the frozen pork chops in my freezer and stuff like that but it was not the same. I needed something unusual.

Then one night, on Miami Beach, a drunk driver hit a statue of an Indian sitting on his horse, holding a large fish high above his head. (could I make this up?) I was a cop and got the call. The only damage to the statue was the fish broke off and was lying in the bushes. I threw it in the trunk of my car and finished my report. Then the idea hit me.

I took the fish home that night and threw it in my freezer. The next day, before work, I plastered my tongue tightly to the fish and POW, instant gratification. I turned the fish in and a week later the City reconnected it to the Indian. I would proudly chuckle to myself every time I passed it. If you're ever in Miami Beach, check out the Indian and know my tongue has been there. Is that awesome, or what? Except for when I tongued a glacier, it was the best entry in my journal. Why is there a statue of an Indian holding a fish on Miami Beach? I don't have a clue.

So there you have it. In my older years I have had to drop the hobby, mostly because my tongue is just plain worn out. But from time to time, I will get the urge to "tongue" something. I am currently in negotiation with our town manager, to allow me to stick my tongue to the old school bell next winter. The request didn't faze him. He's heard it all.

I'M MOVING BACK TO MARS

"LET'S TALK TRASH"

I stared at her with great determination and she stared back with equal determination. No one blinked. I had decided this was not going to be another of those "Mexican standoffs" where I lose because nothing happens. I am going to win this, one way or another. There was total and complete silence as we glared at one another. I mean, who does she think she is, anyway?

Finally, I broke the silence. "OK, let's talk trash. No more pussy footin' around. You either do what I tell you or there will be.......trouble. Take off your clothes, now, or I will rip them from your body." Then I saw her blink. "Ah ha," I thought to myself, "She blinked and I have the upper hand. I am winning and she is toast." Then with coldness I have rarely seen in her, she wrapped her arms around her chest and said, "No, you can't make me."

I dropped my head in disappointment, bringing the stare contest to an end. I would have to use more drastic tactics. I hate using force, but sometimes it's the only way. "If you are not standing there naked by the time I count to five, I will personally remove your clothes. I am bigger and stronger than you. I can do this and you are helpless." I hate to use such harsh tactics, but I am the man of the house and I will have my way with her. Getting a four year old into a bathtub should not be this hard.

But since I am no longer a man of violence, I decided to take a different approach and negotiate. "If you take your bath, I will give you ice cream.....or not." Her hands moved from around her chest to her hips. She shifted her weight to one leg and rolled her eyes back. I took that as a good sign. "So whadayasay, little scallywagger, you want ice cream, or not?" Defiantly, she said, "No, I'm not allowed to eat ice cream right before bedtime."

This cannot be happening. I am a great negotiator and she is four years old. I have decades of life experiences under my belt and she has none. Where do I go from here? Then, as though the devil himself were instructing her, she said, "I'm going to tell mommy you said 'let's talk trash.' You're not allowed to say that to me. I'm only four years old. You're going to be in trouble with my mommy when she gets home."

I stared at her with astonishment. I am now on the defense. If this keeps up, I'll be in the bathtub and she'll be eating ice cream. In desperation, I offered, "I'll make you a deal. If you don't tell mommy I said 'let's talk trash,' I won't tell her you ate ice cream before bedtime, but you have to take your bath." She pondered the offer, looking over at the bathtub several times. "OK, but I want the ice cream before my bath, in case mommy comes home early." "It's a deal, but you must promise me you'll take your bath." "I promise." Finally, success!

After we finished our bowls of ice cream, I escorted her to the bathroom. "I don't want to take my bath now. I have a stomachache." "You get in the tub, I'll get the Tums." "No, Poppy, I'm not allowed to take Tums. I'm going to tell mommy you offered me Tums."

Just then I heard the front door open and in walked my

daughter. Relief poured over me. "She didn't get her bath yet? What have you two been doing? Honey, go take your bath, right now." "OK mommy." Obediently, she headed for the bathroom, peeling off clothes along the way.

Moments later I passed the bathroom and looked in to see my granddaughter sitting in the tub. She smiled at me and whispered, "Poppy, I like talking trash with you."

I AM NOT MAKING THIS UP

Well, Maybe a Little

Let's suppose you are a normal thinking person who decides to visit the state of Florida. Here are a few tips to help you come back alive. Warning: Do not go there in the summer without special heat proof shoes and a gallon of SPF3000 sun screen.

The first thing you will notice after arriving in the Sunshine State is that everyone is driving at least 20 mph over the speed limit. Be aware that if you don't want to participate in this activity, you are at great risk. Floridians consider any person driving the speed limit to be a menace on the road. Also note that most Florida drivers who do not have a criminal record, about 60%, have a permit to carry a concealed weapon, usually an AK47 semiautomatic rifle with a laser scope. The other 40%, the felons, are also carrying guns, but they don't need those pesty permits.

Floridians dislike people who drive the speed limit and since you probably will be the only person on the road who

FRED WOOLDRIDGE

is not armed, I suggest bullet proof glass for your car before entering the state. The alternative is to participate in Florida's famous SOD program. SOD stands for "Speed or Die."

Let's say you are a SOD participant and decide to drive 75mph on a posted 55mph highway. You are tooling along in the left lane, thinking that because of your excessive speed, no one will want to pass. Suddenly, without warning, there is a SOD participant who wants to drive 90mph and you are in his way. You can be pulled over by a Trooper and given a ticket for not yielding. Stay out of the left lane if you don't want a ticket for not yielding to speeders doing 90. Is Florida a great state or what?

Also new on the books this year is a fun new law giving special rights to citizens who do not want to flee from criminals anymore. In the past, citizens had to weenie out and run when being attacked by the bad guys. Criminals who are in your home and just want to leave with a few of your belongings are now at great risk. Citizens are allowed to defend their castle, whether it be home, car or skate board and can actually shoot it out with crooks, all with the blessings of Governor Jeb Bush, who is Billy, the Kid, reincarnated.

Floridians are elated with this new law because they no longer have to drag dead criminals from their front yards back into the house and put kitchen knives in their hands before calling the police. It's a lot less messy and they don't have to get the rugs cleaned.

I mention this because, as a visitor, you could accidentally be shot. Let's say a Floridian cuts you off, acing you out of

I'M MOVING BACK TO MARS

your parking spot at the super market. Since this happens about 7000 times a day per parking lot, pay attention here. You decide to walk over to the driver and tell him how rude he was in cutting you off. The driver thinks you are invading his castle (the car) and decides he is at risk. POW, you go home in a box and the Floridian continues his shopping but only after keying your car.

If you're going to be in Florida for any length of time, you may want to join in the excitement and get your own concealed weapon permit. Here's how. When you show up at the court house, you must demonstrate you are breathing. Sadly as this may seem, several years ago Florida stopped issuing gun permits and voting cards to dead people. Once you have proven you are alive, say the following words. "I drive I-95 regularly." POW, You're signed up.

No need for any special gun training or stupid stuff like that. They will make you promise to read a booklet on the law which says you no longer have to drag criminals into your house after shooting them.

Well, that's it for visiting Florida. I will soon report on secret IQ tests given to North Carolina's Department of Transportation supervisors. Stay tuned because this is really, really scary.

KITTY HAWK, THE SLUT

Our family once owned a 15 pound dachshund who thought her only mission in life was to hunt down and kill everything it could get into her mouth. After destroying several thousand lizards, dozens of rabbits, opossums and cute little chipmunks, she was able to sneak into my daughter's bedroom, break open a bird cage and attack her parakeet.

My daughter grieved for weeks. We had a formal funeral in the back yard, complete with soft music, a headstone and flowers. I did the singing, if you can imagine. After waiting a respectful amount of time, I headed for the pet store to buy her another bird. After looking at all the ho-hum parakeets on display, I spotted this magnificent pearl colored cockatiel in the back of the store.

I thought, "Bigger is better. My daughter will be thrilled with this beauty". I presented her with the bird but she was not impressed, especially after it bit her several times. In fact, no one in the family liked this bird, including me. The store wouldn't take it back, so guess what? I got stuck with it. To this day, I am not quite sure why I named her Kitty Hawk.

Mind you, I like birds a lot. But I like the kind that fly wild and poop in the woods, not in a cage, or on my shirt..... or worse, on my sandwich. (Don't ask!) After Kitty Hawk had lived with us.... Oops, I mean me, for about a year, I could take no more. I offered it to all my friends who laughed at me. Then, I heard about the "bird lady." Supposedly she would adopt any bird who needed a home.

I made the call. "How ode is dis bird?" she asked with a heavy German accent. "Very young," I responded, "I've only had her a year." "Dis bird comes mit cage?" she asked. "Ya, Ya." "Bring da bird mit cage, food and ten dollars. Ve'll see."

It was a modest home way out in the western part of Broward County, Florida. The house was spotless inside because there was not a bird in sight. I began to wonder. Then she escorted Kitty Hawk and I through her home and out into the backyard. I was shocked.

It was immense and set up like a tropical paradise. Two oversized Tiki huts sat just beyond the pool and, at first glance, I would guess I was looking at over a hundred birds and not one of them in a cage. Beyond her yard, nothing but dense vegetation. There were birds at the wet bar, birds basking by the pool, birds in the bird bath. Bird poop was everywhere.

"Vot is dis Kitty Hawk name? Vot is dat mean?" Embarrassed a little, I said. "Ha, oh that, it was my daughter's idea. You know how kids are. Why don't any of these birds fly away?"

The bird lady left for just a moment and returned with one glove and a pair of scissors. She reached in the cage and Kitty Hawk chomped down hard on the glove. Unfazed, she pulled the bird from the cage and whacked away at her wings.

Kitty Hawk was just beginning to get comfortable with her clipped status and surroundings when Tony arrived, a grayer version of Kitty Hawk. You could tell that Tony was "in the mood" as he began strutting his stuff in front of her, kind of like our politicians do right before elections. My baby girl was a virgin and would have nothing to do with Tony. I was so proud of her. Anyway, I decided, in spite of Tony, this was a good thing. Kitty Hawk would live with the bird lady.

About 6 months later I called her to check on Kitty Hawk. "Slut, dis bird is a slut." She raged on. "She has three children, all have different fathers. Your slut bird won't leave the boys alone. You could send more money?" There was silence as my shock wore off. "Hello, hello, I can't hear a word you said." Hmm, must have gotten disconnected. I'll try again later, like in twenty years.

CHAPTER TWO
DEAR FRED

Dear Fred:

I am having trouble with my boyfriend. We have been going together for several years and I just can't get him to commit and take our relationship to the next level. He has moved into my spacious home, doesn't have to work because of my large income and he treats my maid and butler like they are trash. I am at wits end on what to do.

Practically out of Patience

Dear PooP:

You have lots of company. There are hordes of women out there who can't get their boyfriends to the next level, mostly because men don't have a clue what that means. Once our basic needs are met, we go into "status quo" mode and we don't do levels. Don't forget what planet we are from.

You are obviously not doing enough to further this relationship. Try leaving the toilet seat up for awhile, buy him a new fishing pole and keep lots of beer in the frig. Oh yes, I almost forgot, fire the help and hire a maid and butler that are not so trashy.

Dear Fred:

My husband of thirty years hasn't found out yet but I know it is only a matter of time. It started last summer. At first it was innocent enough, only an extra bag of bird seed not intended for the birds. It was love at first sight. After that I couldn't help myself. I did anything to keep him coming back day after day. He's the strong silent type but so gentle with me. After first frost last year he disappeared. I was heartbroken but hid my pain from my husband, Carl.

This year we came back to our mountain home. All the beds had been slept in and all the porridge bowls dirty in the sink. It was unbearable to keep my secret joy as the police took the report. Today there is a neighborhood watch. What am I to do? The love of my life is a fugitive. My neighbor, a retired SWAT officer, is loaded for bear and every broken branch sends my heart racing into my throat.

What am I to do? The love I have for my husband binds me to the past but this new love is now a year old and still burns hot. Where to spend the winter? Do I take the leap and spend the next six months nestled in the bliss of my honey's arms? Awaiting your response as I cut my golden curls I remain

Unbearable Feelings

Dear Space Cadet:

Here are a few thoughts right off the top of my head. First, never date anyone who eats bird seed and second, never live next door to a retired SWAT guy.

I hope Carl is wired tighter than you are. Reading between the lines, I assume you are interested in dumping Carl, who must be a Saint, and run off with someone who disappears after first frost, breaks into your house when you're not home, leaves dirty dishes in the sink and sleeps around in every bed you have. Then he shows up in spring wanting to be fed.

Keep far away from the strong and silent types. They never say anything and life can get real boring, although they are great to have around for heavy lifting. Retired SWAT commandos will make you a nervous wreck, although it seems you might already be there. My hard and fast rule of love is: "Never sleep with anyone who wears camouflage paint to bed."

Wolves will howl at noon before I could ever come up with a solution to your dilemma. Maybe you could get Carl to eat bird seed, I don't know. One thing for sure, you are a scary person! If I were you, I would not spend the winter nestled in the bliss of your honey's arms but, instead, check into the Heavenly Hills Rest Home.

PS: Are you sure you don't live in Gatlinburg?

Dear Fred:

I know this is none of my business but I have noticed you are getting up in years and I was wondering if you have discovered the wonders of Viagra. (Blush)

Yours Truly,

Miss Nosey

Dear none of your business (Blush):

Puh-leeze, we are trying to run a wholesome, clean cut, family oriented newspaper here. We never use that word around the office, much less print it in this newspaper. We prefer to call it the "V word."

Your question is a hard one to answer because it is sooooo personal.

First, for those of you who have been living on the moon, let me explain that "V" is a drug which causes... Aaaaa... well, let's just say, sexual excitement. (Here, picture me blushing again) "V" was discovered by accident when scientists, looking for a better way to thin blood, overdosed their guinea pig patient, who became ... well... you know, excited... and wound up chasing the nurse around the bed several hundred times.

This new discovery has been a wonderful thing for old geezers who no longer have to grind up those tiny little Spanish flies and sprinkle them in their chicken soup. They just pop the little blue pill into their mouths and, POW, they are Superman. The only thing I have found more important than using "V" that older women look for in a man is whether he can drive at night.

I interviewed one older, single man on Main Street about his use of "V." He said, "It puts a lot of lead in my pencil, but I just don't have anyone to write to at this time."

There are many problems and much concern in our communities across the country over the use of "V." Women everywhere are dumping their twenty something husbands and boyfriends and hooking up with old codgers who are overdosing on "V."

As for me, the answer really is none of your business. Let's just say I threw my grinder away a long time ago and I have very thin blood.

Dear Fred:

I am having eight people for dinner and my husband and I are arguing over whether to serve the salad first and then the entree or just sit the whole dinner on the table at once. He says serving the salad first is much too formal for our atmosphere. He is really being a persistent jerk on this issue. What do you think?

Salad Now On The Table

Dear S.N.O.T.T.:

First off, never invite eight people for dinner because, including you and your grumpy husband, that makes a total of ten. Since you only have a table setting for eight, two people are going to have to eat off the plates you got from the last Bi Lo promotion. Then again, the road you live on is in such poor condition, expect most people without four wheel drive cars won't show anyway.

Secondly, don't worry about the atmosphere. Keep the room temperature at seventy and don't serve cocktails outside if it is snowing. Practically no one I know of ever refuses to go to a dinner party because of poor atmospheric conditions. Check the weather the day before, which won't help you much.

Also, never take your husband to Italy for fine dining. There's a good chance that he will get his salad served at the end of the meal and you will have to unscrew him from the ceiling.

If your bone-headed husband really wants to turn this into a major tiff then you must realize that a mere salad is not worth all this arguing and bickering. Simply send him to his room until everyone has finished your succulent garden repast and then serve his salad with his entrée. Remind him that he is in charge of the lawn mower and you are in charge of the kitchen.

When desert is served, make sure he gets an extra small portion. When he gives you that icy glare from across the table and then looks down at his desert, ask him if he enjoyed his salad.

Remember, training people from Mars is a never ending process.

Dear Fred:

I am liddle and my mommy said I could rite you a question. Josh and Buster are in my class and they told me there is no Santa Claus. I think they are rite 'cause I saw him once at school when he wasn't dressed up and I think he might be a fake Santa. Is there really a Santa? I am not allowed to beet them up 'cause I am a girl.

Tish

Dear Tish:

Way back when I was liddle, maybe a hundred and fifty years ago, I was told by a kid named Ed Crawley that there was no Santa Claus. I am still mad at him. Finally I got up enough nerve to ask my Mom and here is what she said.

"If you don't believe in Santa, then he will be sad. He will still bring you toys because he will always love you but he will do it with a sad face and a pouty lip. So you think about that and make your own decision. Do you want Santa to be sad or happy?" Turns out she was a wise mom because I still believe in Santa, even today.

FRED WOOLDRIDGE

Just because someone tells you their beliefs, doesn't necessary mean it's true. People used to believe the world was flat, but that does not make it so. In fact, if you didn't think it was flat, you were considered nuts. Today, if you think the world is flat, you are some kind of nut case.

Just because some people don't want to believe in Santa doesn't mean he doesn't exist. He is more than just a big jolly fat man who brings you toys on Christmas. Santa is about unconditional love and giving. He is unselfish as he doesn't expect anything in return for all his work. Just believe in him and love him, nothing more.

There are people in the world that think there isn't a God. Well guess what, Tish. There is a God and just because some people think there isn't, doesn't make it so.

If you are a Christian child then you know that on Christmas we celebrate the birth of Jesus Christ. Santa and Jesus have one big thing in common. They both give of themselves unconditionally. All they ever ask for is love and belief in return. As your parents probably already taught you, Jesus gave of himself, and his life, so we can live forever. Saint Nick, as he is sometimes called, gives us gifts at Christmas to remind us of Christ's gift to mankind. As long as there is unconditional love and giving there will always be a Santa Claus.

So the choice is yours, Tish. Do you want to believe in Santa or do you want to be like Josh and Buster? I

I'M MOVING BACK TO MARS

think you are going to be like me and believe in Santa your whole life.

Dear Fred:

You must help me polish my driving manners and at the same time be effective. My problem is how to drive to Franklin and back faster than 25 miles per hour.

Every time I go, there seems to be a slowpoke ahead of me. They do not seem to notice the turn outs cut especially for them and I cannot seem to get them to use them. If you are going to suggest blinking my headlights and honking the horn, I have already tried that and the drivers ahead of me get annoyed and slow down. I am not suggesting that I want to drive more than 45 mph, but 20 is just ridiculous.

I certainly realize that the road is scenic and curvy; but there are those of us that have to make that trip often and cannot dawdle. Help me please....

Sincerely,

Mytee Peeved

Dear MP:

Ha, if you lived in Miami, where I used to make a living, I could have your problem solved in seconds. Down there they use the "bump and point" system to get pesty tourists out of the way. They lightly bump the car in front of them to get their attention and when the

FRED WOOLDRIDGE

tourists look in their mirrors, they're looking down the barrel of a gun. Works every time. But if you think you can get away with that up here, better think again. I guarantee you you'll be in the clink before you can say "How much are the tickets to the policeman's ball?

I am the last person to be polishing you up on driving manners. When behind the wheel, I suffer from the "Top Gun" syndrome, which I can't go into right now, but I am on medications for it. I have been driving the gorge road since the late sixties. When I used to have a less hazardous job than writing for this paper, my main office was at "Bust Your Butt Falls" where I jumped off of cliffs everyday. I share your frustrations.

Here is a list of things I have suggested in the past to help the Department of Transportation arrive at a solution. (1) Sedative stations at each end of the road. You pull over, take a mild sedative and resume your travel. You won't get there any faster but you just won't care. (2) Offer free orange juice at pull off areas. That is sure to work because tourists will do anything to get their hands on a 2 ounce cup of free orange juice. (3) Free chauffeur service for tourists. Cars with out-of-town license plates would be required to pull over and have a local person drive them to the other end. Again, sedatives will be offered, only this time to tourists.

The State did not cotton to any of my ideas, so back to the drawing board. Here is my latest idea which they probably won't like either.

I'M MOVING BACK TO MARS

Last year I uncovered and reported to our readers the testing of a US Government secret weapon which fires dead roosters at airplane windshields. Don't ask, just take my word for it. These babies are now on sale from the Pentagon for a mere 1.2 mil, which is a good deal considering you get six free birds with the package. The introduction of this new weapon gives new meaning to the term "shooting the bird."

Bring on the "Gallus Domesticus" cannon. With one of the beauties strapped to the hood of your car, you are king of the gorge road. Here's how she works. Roll up behind a tourist and toot your horn real friendly like. Once you are sure they are looking in their mirror, fire a dead rooster at their back window. POW. While still in a state of shock, they quickly pull over and let you pass. As an added incentive the tourists can race back and pick up the bird for dinner if they wish. Kinda' like road kill for city slickers.

Dear Fred.

I recently sent my girlfriend, Loretta, a dozen roses in hopes of moving our relationship to the next level.

I was real happy when she called and said she loved me. I asked her if it was the flowers that made her see me in a new light. She said it was the card that was attached that did the trick. She's into handwriting analysis and said that after she analyzed my handwriting she realized that I am her

FRED WOOLDRIDGE

perfect match, her soul-mate. Only problem is the woman at the florist was the one that wrote the card. I ordered the flowers over the phone.

What should I do?

Freaked Out Over Loretta

Dear F.O.O.L.:

Oh boy, you have already made so many mistakes I don't know if I can safely bail you out of this one. Rule #1: Never, never, never send flowers to a woman unless you are in real, double Dutch, down in the dirt, serious, big time trouble. Rule #2: Never date anyone who is a handwriting specialist. She probably has already analyzed your life line and knows your astrological sign. (I hope you're not a Feces.)

People who do these things are very analytical and you will never have a minute's rest with this gal. She will always be asking, "What exactly did you mean by that comment?" They also ask "How do you think that makes me feel?" and other scary girl type questions. My best advice is to run.

But if I can't talk you out of trashing your life with this woman, here is what I would do. Find the girl at the florist who wrote the card. Pay her an enormous sum of money to give you pages and pages of her handwriting. Then practice, practice, practice until your script is exactly like hers. Use the onion skin/tracing method. It worked great for me in the sixth grade when I needed a note from home to get out of trouble.

Once your relationship has reached the fatal, last level, (The big "M") smash your writing hand with a large mallet and tell her it was an accident. I realize this might be a bit drastic but we are desperate here. When the bandages come off, complain to your new wife that your handwriting is different since the accident and then you can return to your old scribble. By then, it will be too late for her... and you.

And remember, this could have all been avoided if you had just **not** sent the roses.

Dear Fred:

We have a beautiful young daughter still living with us who brings home the dirtiest and sleaziest boyfriends I have ever seen. Our Donna is just finishing college and plans to become a veterinarian. Her current boyfriend, Anthony, is an unemployed high school drop-out who doesn't work and is just a bum. Anthony hangs around our home all day, eats our food and has made himself a part of our family. We don't want him around but we don't want to hurt Donna's feelings. Please, what are we to do?

Down On Anthony, from Auburn

Dear D.O.A. :

You have contacted the right person for your dilemma as I am an expert at getting rid of boyfriends. I also have a beautiful, kind of young daughter who has since married. Amazingly, I still get hate mail from her ex-boyfriends, but that's another story.

FRED WOOLDRIDGE

Your letter also brings back old times for me because it's exactly like the one my mother-in-law wrote to Ann Landers when my wife brought me home for the first time. Nah, only kidding. She actually liked me if you can believe that.

The good news is your daughter will eventually move out of your home and take Anthony, the dirt bag, with her. Since trying to break them up will only drive them closer together and since you really can't do anything about Anthony anyway, here is what I suggest as an interim plan.

Limburger cheese is the solution to your problem. Lots and lots of Limburger cheese. Unless he is of Belgium descent, he probably won't like this stuff. Leave a large slab of this smelly concoction on the kitchen table. When Anthony asks what's for lunch, shove the cheese under his nose. You will find, not only will Anthony reject your lunch offer, he will continuously be checking the soles of his shoes. You can actually eat this stuff if your take two cigarette filters and shove them up your nostrils before you clamp your teeth around a Limburger and pickle sandwich. But don't tell Anthony.

For dinner, Limburger lasagna and heavy on the garlic. Have you ever smelled a combination of Limburger and garlic mixed together, baking in the oven? It's worse than Saddam's breath. Forty minutes of that and Anthony will be reeling, looking for the door. Remember, the way to Anthony's permanent exit is though his nose and eventually, his stomach.

I'M MOVING BACK TO MARS

Next, wait until Anthony takes his nap in your favorite easy chair and then sneak outside and slap another slab of Limburger on the exhaust manifold of his car. He won't be back for days because he'll be afraid to start his car. While he's away, buy a Rottweiler who doesn't like anyone, especially Anthony. Problem solved.

Dear Fred:

I am only three credit hours away from receiving my degree in engineering but I am struggling in a math course I am taking. Please review this formula and if you can add a hypothesis, please help as I am about to flunk this class. Here it is.

Using L as a constant, consider L pi = the ratio of 27 minus the circumference of M as a radical to the 3rd power. I have approached this problem using several theorems, including the Quantum Four and Schlepp methods but nothing works for me. I remain bogged down. You might just be my last hope.

Stumped at MIT

Dear SMIT:

You are soooooo lucky to have written me with this problem as I am an expert in this particular field. Don't take this as an insult, but I can tell by the wimpy tone of your question that you definitely are **not** a member of the "I Phelta Thi" fraternity. You guys are all the same,

FRED WOOLDRIDGE

walking around with that Albert Einstein look on your face. I'll bet you haven't kissed a girl since high school, if then. I know your type. You sleep with your slide rule and eat Shredded Wheat for dinner just because someone told you to loosen up a little. Now you need a guy like me to bail you out. Well, I have been saving guys like you for years and I can be of great assistance, if you just follow my plan.

Do not consider using L as a constant and never use the Schlepp method when you have a perfectly good car sitting in front of your dorm. In fact forget about L and Quantum Four altogether and find a smart girl in your class who is making A's. Even if she is uglier than a Highland's public restroom, make a move on her and do whatever it takes to get into her study group.

Next, take off that stupid looking hat you've been wearing to class and do not, I repeat, do not have a half dozen pens stuck in your shirt pocket when you meet her for the first time. Definitely no pencil behind your ear either, at least not for the first date. Don't even bring up math. Talk about girl things and show lots of interest in her. Ask about her mother; stupid stuff like that. Then, when the moment is just right, pour a glass of her favorite wine, put on some soft jazz background music, make sure the fire is crackling in the fireplace and then, and only then, snuggle up close to her on the couch and whisper softly in her ear as you secretly pull out your calculator, "What is the answer to number six?"

Dear Fred:

I am a 15-year-old girl and have been dating a 17-year-old boy for several months. I'll call him Bruce. My problem is every time we go out to eat, Bruce orders steak and potatoes. Neither of us have a great deal of money to spend, but I usually have to pay for the meal most of the time and I end up having to order a salad because that's all I can afford. I'm thinking of breaking up over this. Do you think I should?

Miss Skinny

Dear MS:

Never break up with someone just because he is a good old fashioned meat and tater guy. They are a rare group these days with all the food fads that are out there. Tofu, bean sprouts, twigs and berries are the "in" food today. A recent study has revealed that M & T (that's short for meat and tater) guys make good boyfriends, but are declining in numbers.

All that protein builds big muscles, which is what girls like to see. I always say, "If you can snag an M & T guy, hang on to him at all costs." There is nothing more vitalizing than having a 16 ounce Sirloin steak coursing through your veins while working out at the gym. Be thankful that he doesn't eat Sushi. Have you ever smelled the breath of people who eat raw fish dunked in that awful smelling gobbly-gook?

I realize none of this important information is helping

FRED WOOLDRIDGE

you with your problem so I would try several things with Bruce before breaking up. First, get a job after school so you can afford to pay for Bruce's meals and maybe occasionally have a steak yourself. Next, start cooking for him at home. Supermarket steaks are a lot cheaper than restaurant beef. If he balks at this, back off immediately and tell him you will also take in ironing to earn extra bucks to buy steaks and taters.

You must be the envy of every girl at school. I'm impressed. Tell your girlfriends I'm a meat and tater guy myself, but I am also spoken for.

Not So Dear Fred:

I am a refined, intelligent lady who reads your articles and I find you to be the most arrogant, obnoxious and mean spirited person I think I have ever known. I wouldn't vote for you, even if you ran for dog catcher. I can't stand you. How did you get like that?

Angry

Dear Angry:

Well, I am not running for dog catcher and normally I don't like to respond to questions with sexual overtones, but in this case, I will make an exception. After all, "normal" is not in my vocabulary.

Everyone who has seen the movie "My Big Fat Greek Wedding" knows that all words come from Greek origin. In this case the word "arrogant" comes from the Greek slang term, or group of words "arroganous manarrous" which means sensuous mannerisms and feelings for an object. This most often happens with men and their guns, but that's another story. As a female, your use of this word connotes, in Greek translation, a sexual fascination with my words in print.

Furthermore, the word "obnoxious", in Greek translation, means noxious-pladedious or, I want to grope or touch an object that belongs to a person like me who puts words in print.

This fetish you have is more common among women who voted in Palm Beach, Florida, during the presidential race. Closing the voting booth curtain behind them, they caressed the candidate's names in front of them and were overhead saying, "Bless me, Father, for I have sinned." If you are from Palm Beach, I can't help you.

But if you are from elsewhere, I can temporarily relieve you of your sexual fantasies. Here's how. Make an appointment with me immediately and I will let you come over and fondle my computer......as long as you wear gloves and my wife is home. That should hold you for awhile.

Oh, I almost forgot to tell you how I got like this. It takes years of hard work. First, get a job as a policeman in Miami and stay there 28 years. That will get you well underway. Then spend the next 14 years dangling from a rope on the cliffs, followed by a controversial column for a newspaper. Pow, you become like me. I am soooooo impressed that you want to emulate me.

FRED WOOLDRIDGE

Dear Fred:

When should I plant my spring bulbs?
Mr. Duh:

Dear Duh:

You haven't supplied me with enough information to consider answering you. I will need the wattage of each bulb, which spring you got them from and, of course, the time of year you want to plant them. Sheeeesh.

Dear Fred:

My husband and I play bridge with you and your wife at a large game during the summer. We have gotten to know you both quite well. For that reason, I have gone to great lengths to hide my identity, so don't try to find me. Here's my question.

Your wife is such a dignified, cultured and respectful person. How on earth she ever wound up marrying a weird person like you is beyond me.

Signed, very undercover

Hello Janice:

Good to hear from you. How are you and Arnie doing? You must have forgotten that I used to be a gumshoe in my other life. Finding you was so easy. I just traced your bogus e mail address to a fictitious location in South Africa (Hey, that was clever.) and then went to Google.com, who knows everything about everyone, and followed the money trail right to your doorstep. You have hidden your identity about as good as you play bridge. Remember, the money trail will always give you up.

Also, I might add, you have a lot of nerve calling me weird when I happen to know that your Arnie likes to wear his rubber chicken suit around the house, a leftover from when he worked for Cluckie's Fried Chicken. Rumor has it that he also does interesting things with hard boiled eggs.

But since I am a professional, I will not stoop to your level with insults and unfounded allegations. I will rise above it all and give you a legitimate answer.

A zillion years ago when the little missus and I were first married, she would say to me all the time, "You are a scary man." Then, as time passed and we changed, I began to say to her, "You are also a scary woman." The truth is, on the surface, she is a dignified, cultured and respectful person. But underneath all that, my better half is just as zany as I am. As it turns out, we both have only one oar in the water, but as long as we are together in the same boat, we get to where we are going. We feed off each other. Inside the confines of our home, there is always laughter. We laugh at everything and I am always astounded at some of the wild things she comes up with, for my ears only, of course. It is one of several bonds that glue us together.

FRED WOOLDRIDGE

So, Miss undercover smarty pants who thought she could pull this off, let me give you a little advice to improve your relationship with Arnie. You should try to be a little more like him and cater more to his needs, like maybe investing in your own rubber chicken outfit. You already have the proper physique to pull it off.

See you at bridge this summer.

CHAPTER THREE
CHILDREN'S STORIES

MANUEL CARLOS RODRIGUEZ MENDEZ-MACEDO AND THE THREE BEARS

I have just finished my first children's book, specially designed for those savvy, streetwise tots who were born and raised in Miami. Read it slowly, using your best singsong voice, like when you talk to toddlers, or old people, like me.

Once upon a time, there were threeeeee bears, papa bear, mamma bear, and the very lovable, but extremely obese (that means fat) baby bear. Oh, what is a bear, you ask? I forgot you live in Miami. A bear is a large hairy animal that hoards all the food he can find and leaves none for anyone else, kind of like Fidel Castro, only without the fatigue cap.

The three bears were tooling around Miami (here, I show a picture of three cool looking bears in a Jaguar convertible) when they happen upon the home of Manuel Carlos Rodriguez Mendez-Macedo. Let's just call him Manny to save ink. Looking in the window, the bears see that Manny isn't home, so papa bear, using his latest state of the art burglary tools, breaks into the house. (In the original version, a little girl named Goldilocks commits the felony.) As your parents have already taught you, breaking and entering of an unoccupied dwelling is a third degree felony in Florida, but you are not afraid for baby bear because you have read my publication, "Special Treatment for Child Felons," and know that baby bear will only get timeout, if caught.

Once inside the house, the bears head straight for the liquor cabinet. Papa bear tastes the Jamaican Rum. "This rum is too strong." Mamma bear then tastes the Grand Marnier. "This is too weak." Baby bear then breaks the seal on a bottle of Louie XIV brandy and says, "This brandy is just right," and drinks it alllll up. (Here, pictures of baby bear holding a brandy snifter bigger than his head.)

Next, off to the kitchen where they find three bowls of paella on the table. Tasting from the first bowl, papa bear says, "This paella is too spicy." Mamma bear samples the second bowl. "This paella is too mild." Baby bear is now having trouble with his motor control from drinking the brandy, but struggles to sip from the third bowl. "This is just right" and eats it alllll up.

Then baby bear announces "I am sleepy" (who wouldn't be) and the three head for the bedrooms. Papa bear finds his bed too hard; mamma bear announces hers is too soft and baby bear could care less about comfort and just wants to lie down and get some sleep.

While the bears sleep, Manny comes home and sees that his house has been broken into. He finds the empty bottle of Louie XIV as well as the empty paella bowls. He screams out in anger, reaching for his .357 Magnum revolver. See my

I'M MOVING BACK TO MARS

publication, "Fun with Guns in Miami," which gives colorful illustrations of most of the guns currently being aimed at you in South Florida.

Manny's scream awakens mamma and papa bear but they are unable to wake up baby bear as he is too blitzed on paella and brandy to budge. Leaving him, they leap out the bedroom window. Again, do not become alarmed. Read my handbook "Escaping the Child Welfare Department Before Getting Killed" and you will see that baby bear is going to be OK.

After doing the "Someone has been sleeping in my bed" bit twice, Manny comes across baby bear, still zonked out, and decides to call the police. While he is away, baby bear awakens, finds his parents gone and heads for the bedroom window. Baby bear is too fat to fit through the window opening and gets stuck. (Here, an inside picture of baby bear's great big fanny stuck in the window. Be sure to point and laugh.)

Meanwhile, Manny is so relieved that the bears didn't find his cocaine stash that he decides to let baby bear go and not call the police. Baby bear is eventually reunited with his parents and they all live happily ever after.

No more burglaries for baby bear until he loses some weight and completes the 12 step program. And I always like to leave parents who buy my books with a statement of moral logic, like "Never leave the house with a bear behind."

FRED WOOLDRIDGE

THE STORY OF WHINNY, THE POOP

(A bear bones drama)

Here is another of my interesting children's stories, specially written for those bratty little city slicker types from Atlanta and Miami who visit Highlands, North Carolina, and want to know the real poop about bears. Just like life in the big city, this story does not have a happy ending, so prepare your listener for a pouty mouth. (Maybe you should practice pouty mouths with your little urchin.)

Once upon a time there were threeeeee bears. There was papa bear, who was always out chasing younger female bears, mamma bear, who was stressed over Highland's growth, and her little baby bear named Whinny. Because Whinny was born next to the Highlands Sewer and Treatment Plant, she decided to call him, Whinny, the Poop.

In the beginning, life was wonderful for Poop. He would while away his summer days sitting at the edge of the treatment plant, watching treated waste water from Highlands' toilets flow into the beautiful river. One day, Whinny asked his Mamma, "Why do humans play and fish in the river and I am not allowed to even set foot near it? Not fair." "Life is not fair," she would always respond and reminded him that humans just didn't know any better.

Mamma bear took the opportunity to tell Whinny more about humans. "Always keep away from these dangerous creatures. They are the only critters on the planet that kill for fun and they just love to cut down trees and pour black gooey

I'M MOVING BACK TO MARS

stuff on the forest floor so they can go fast in their cars.

One day, papa bear came home and announced, "We are moving to an empty cave at the Highlands Country Club. Pack your stuff." Mama bear was thrilled and said, "We'll dine on Russian caviar and everyone there has a bird feeder in their backyard, but what happened to the family who lived there?" Papa bear laughed, "They couldn't take the growth, the noise and the parties. People constantly clinking those wine glasses was more than they could handle."

So that night Whinny and his parents headed for their new digs. Whinny turned to take a last look at the cave where he was born. He would miss the treatment plant, the roar of water over the dam and the tourists making fools of themselves in the river.

Once everyone was settled into their new surroundings, papa bear headed out to check on the female bears around the club while mama bear and Whinny made lists of the homes they would raid. Each evening Whinny would head for the back decks to eat from their bird feeders. Whinny raided so many decks on one evening, the expression "Poop Deck" was invented. Life was sooooo good.

Winter eventually came and it was time to hibernate. Most of the humans had left the club and pickens' were slim anyway. That is when it happened. Just after dawn on a bitter cold February morning, Whinny and his parents were awakened by the roar of bulldozers and humans in pickup trucks. "They're building a house right over our cave. We'll have to move," papa bear angrily complained.

FRED WOOLDRIDGE

That night, Whinny and his parents left their cave in search of a place to live. It would be impossible to find a cave in the dead of winter since most were occupied or had been covered over by humans. For the first time in Whinny's life, he was homeless. (Here, do a pouty mouth with your brat.) Whinny and his family roamed the forest for days looking for housing and Whinny was exhausted from the search. This is how the expression "pooped out" came to be. Even the cave at the treatment plant was occupied by a bunch of red neck bears from Dollywood, Tennessee.

Finally, mama bear announced, "We have no choice, we'll have to move to Gatlinburg and get jobs working for the Indians, entertaining vacationers." Papa bear was shocked. "Ah, not me, I'm going to head out. See ya; have a nice life." This proved to be a bad decision as papa bear was eventually captured by trappers, posing as female bears. He is currently wearing a dunce hat and riding a motor scooter for the Bear Bones Circus and Freak Show.

Everyone lost track of Poop and his mom. Rumor has it she went to Gatlinburg and her hide is currently for sale in a local gift shop. Whinny supposedly returned to Highlands and broke into a home for the remainder of the winter.

So if you see a young bear on your back deck tonight, be nice. It just might be "The Poop."

I'M MOVING BACK TO MARS

PETER SPAM IN NEVERLAND

Here is another of my wonderful children's stories you can read when you want your little urchin to have terrible nightmares and start sucking his thumb again. It is the story of a little boy named Peter Spam and how he found a place called "Neverland," high in the mountains of North Carolina. After reading this story, I recommend you give your listener a mild sedative.

Once upon a time there was a boy named Peter Spam who was happy living with his mother, father and little sister. Then, one day, Mr. Spam decided it would be just grand if the whole Spam family took a trip to the mountains of North Carolina. So they packed their stuff in the Spam family van and headed out.

But along the way, a very bad thing happened. The Spam's family van slammed into a Ram, badly damaging the Spam's family van. Can you say "Spam's Family Van Slammed into a Ram" real fast, three times? Isn't that fun?

While Peter and his family sat dazed, a fairy appeared before him and said. "Hello little Peter, I am the good fairy, Michael, from Neverland and I am here to help you."

At first, Peter was afraid of Michael because he had very white skin and really looked a lot like "The Joker" from the movie, "Batman." Then, with a wisp of his finger, Michael floated on top of the Spam van and did a great moon walk while doing interesting things with his crotch. "Don't be afraid, I will not harm you. I have millions of dollars and can take care of your family's car repair bills. If you will allow me to sprinkle some pixie dust on you, you will be able to fly like me and we can go to Neverland and have fun together."

Peter looked over at the badly damaged family van and decided he had no choice. He agreed to become a fairy and then Michael said, "Here is my personal check for one million dollars and I will pin it to your dad's shirt since he is still in a daze. Now let's get out of here because I hear the police coming."

With that, Peter and Michael flew away, heading north into the mountains toward Neverland. Along the way Michael told Peter about how he built Neverland. "I did it myself. It used to be a place called Highlands, but they got so caught up in greed and making money that it became an unhappy place to live. I bought the whole town and converted it into Neverland. Now there is no greed, just me, my pixie friends and my money."

"It sounds wonderful, but where do I live," Peter asked? "All my friends live with me at the Neverland Castle. I have a giant bed where everyone sleeps. We will have so much fun. I will give you colorful pajamas, interesting books with pictures to look at, and best of all, Neverland happy juice."

Now little Peter was beginning to worry a bit about this guy, Michael. He also worried about his parents and sister. But what could he do? He had agreed to accompany Michael to Neverland. "I think I want to check on my family," Peter said. "That's silly. Here's another check for one million dollars you can cash at the Neverland Bank when we get there."

I'M MOVING BACK TO MARS

Once Peter got settled in at the Neverland Castle, he put on his colorful pajamas, looked at a few books and was on his third glass of Neverland happy juice when there was a loud bang on the bedroom door. The door flew open and in walked the police, accompanied by Peter's parents and sister. They had a search warrant.

Then the police said, "The car accident was only a dream. You are under the spell of Michael, the pixie, and I'm glad we got here in time. As they carried Michael away in chains, Michael said, "Don't worry, I always beat the charges. I'll be right back." Then Michael's bodyguards escorted Peter's parents out of Neverland and they never saw their son again. (Here, another pouty mouth and sad face.)

Years later, someone spotted Peter singing and dancing at a local Neverland nightclub. He was thin, had pasty skin and was teaching customers how to do the moon walk. Of course, he was wearing his colorful pajamas.

Now isn't that a fun story? Do you want to wear a pair of colorful pajamas?

FRED WOOLDRIDGE

BIG RED RIDING LEAVES THE HOOD

Here is another of my famous children's stories, especially designed to entertain those sophisticated big city type three to five year olds who are bored with all the unrealistic blah, blah, blah they're dishing out these days. Remember to hold your little whipper-snapper close for the scary part. Speak real slowly, like when you're trying to explain to your yard man exactly what you want done.

Once upon a time there was a little girl named Red Riding...... well, maybe she was not so little since she was only ten years old and already tipping the scales at 150 pounds. Red loved fast food and ate it all the time. The kids at school called her Big Red. Can you say Big Red?

Red lived in a scary place called Atlanta, where practically everyone was divorced and no one spoke to anyone because they were too busy making money and adjusting their 401K plans.

One day, while her mother was at work, Big Red decided to leave her neighborhood (the hood) and visit her Grammy, who lived far, far away and high, high, high in the mountains in a wonderful place called Highlands.

Since there were no fast food restaurants in Highlands, Red decided to buy a six pack of "Big Macs," a full bag of trans fat fries and several chocolate shakes to tide her over until she got home. There are no trains, planes or buses that go to Highlands, so Red had to spend her entire child support payment from her daddy to rent a limo to get there.

I'M MOVING BACK TO MARS

In the meantime, Tubby Arbuckle, a fast food addict himself who lived near Grammy, got wind of Big Red's visit and knew she would arrive with greasy burgers and fries. He also remembered that Grammy would be away the entire day in Cherokee, gambling away her dead husband's hard earned inheritance.

Tubby raced home to put on his Halloween bear costume and after jumping into Grammy's nightgown and hat, waited in her bed for Big Red's arrival.

When she finally arrived, Red spotted the fake bear outfit and knew it must be Tubby, looking to pull off a scam to scarf down her food. She decided to play along. "Oh Grammy, what big ears you have," Red proclaimed, as she pulled a succulent burger from her sack and took a bite, allowing the greasy juices to drip onto Tubby's costume. "The better to hear you eating that wonderful burger. Does it have extra cheese?" Tubby asked.

Big Red pulled ten fries from her bag and shoved them all into her mouth at once. "Oh my, what big eyes you have, Grammy." "The better to see how many fries you have left in your bag. Do you think Grammy could have just one fry?" Tubby asked. "Maybe," Red retorted, holding a single fry over Tubby's mouth which was now wide open. "Maybe not." and pulled it away, shoving it into her mouth.

Tubby could hardly stand the pressure. The smell of the burgers and watching Red eat them was more than he could take. "Grammy has not had lunch yet. Maybe we could have lunch together?" Tubby asked. "Great idea, Grammy.

FRED WOOLDRIDGE

Let me fix you a plate of your favorite broccoli and bean casserole."

That was it. Tubby leaped from the bed and pulled off the bear costume, demanding that Big Red share her food with him. (This is the scary part and it gets a little violent, but nothing worse than what your child sees on the evening news or morning cartoons.)

"Tubby Arbuckle, I knew it was you, you scoundrel. I'm not sharing my food with the likes of you." Red knew she would be no match for Tubby in a tussle, so she grabbed her food and ran, but Tubby was able to tackle her as she ran to the front door. Thinking quick, Red pulled a burger from her bag and tossed it across the room. Acting on instinct, Tubby turned her loose and raced toward the burger, allowing Red to leap into her limo and head for home.

Our story has a happy ending and, of course, everyone lived happily ever after. Big Red returned home safely, eating all her burgers and fries along the way. Tubby got his one free burger and Grammy hit the jackpot at the casino. She just can't figure out how all that grease got on her nightie.

CHAPTER FOUR
SERIOUS STUFF

SHE HAUNTS MY MEMORY

I really dislike writing about my life as a police officer, mostly because that part of my life is over. After twenty-eight years of active police work, I have seen and done it all, but sitting around telling police stories that most people don't believe anyway is not my idea of having fun. Not anymore.

Now I will break my own rule and share a story with you that occurred a long time ago. I want to tell you because I believe you will enjoy it and, unlike most cop stories, this one is worth telling. It is not a story about cops, but a story about people.

In the winter of 1962 I was very much a rookie, still wet behind the ears, as they say. In those years, the police handled all rescue calls and firemen put out fires. Our training was minimal and our equipment primitive. Your chances of surviving a major medical trauma were slim to none. It was just how things were then.

It was an early morning incident, just after roll call. The "Woman down, code 3" signal was typical as the season was

FRED WOOLDRIDGE

in full swing and South Florida was full of visitors, many of them elderly. I arrived at the swanky Miami Beach hotel and lifted the heavy first aid and oxygen kit from my trunk.

A crowd of spectators had formed around a frail, elderly lady who had been placed on the lobby couch. She was an attractive woman, in her seventies, wearing a colorful long sleeved dress and modest jewelry. Her hair was fully gray, with each strand set perfectly in its place. You could tell that, in her younger years, she was a beautiful woman.

I knelt down beside her to administer oxygen as it was apparent by the pale color of her skin she was suffering a heart attack. Her eyes had been closed but when she felt the mask touch her face, she opened them and pushed the mask away. I pulled the mask from her hand and again tried to force oxygen into her lungs but she again pushed the mask away. She reached up and touched my cheek and smiled, looking directly into my eyes. She spoke so softly I could not hear her so I leaned down and put my ear closer to her mouth. Her European accent was thick and I had to pay close attention to understand her. "Officer, it is my time. You can't help me. Please hold me." I pulled away from her and she smiled at me again, reaching to touch my face. She mouthed the words again without speaking. "Please hold me."

Overwhelmed by this, I instinctively lifted her upper torso from the couch and held her tightly. She put her arms around me ever so gently and gave up her life.

Rookies occasionally did cry but not me. I was always able to hold it back. A year later, I would be able to handle this kind of incident with complete indifference, a job hazard.

Later, when the Medical Examiner personnel lifted her limp body into a bag, one of her dress sleeves rode up her arm revealing a tattooed ten digit number on her inner forearm, placed there by the Nazis many years ago. I would later learn from the detective assigned to investigate her death that she had no living relatives. Her husband, children and sister had all been killed in the concentration camps. She had been alone in the world and now she was at peace. I suppose it had been quite some time since anyone had held this pretty lady in their arms. I feel so privileged to have been the last person to have done that.

This happened over forty years ago and I remember it today as vividly as if it were yesterday. It is her smile that haunts me, the feel of her hand on my face, her soft whisper in my ear, her arms sliding from around my back and falling limp. I don't think of her as often as I used to. Time has a way of putting all things in the past. But every now and then, she pops into my mind. It is a pleasant haunting. Someone I knew for only a brief few minutes. I pray that my death will be as gentle and peaceful as hers.

PRAISE THE LORD AND PASS THE A BOMBS

Since the beginning of recorded history, we humans have had this insatiable need to kill each other in the name of God. We are the only species on this planet that does that. History will show that mankind has not advanced very far down through the ages.

If you ask the average person the causes of war and violence, most will say greed and territory. I believe religion tops them all.

Make no mistake of my intent here. I simply refuse to believe that the God I have come to know and love has ever, or will ever, ask humans to kill for Him. But murdering humans in the name of religion or in the name of God has been going on for centuries.

I won't even go into the millions of Hindus and Muslims that are still killing each other over whose religion and God is the right one. Don't have enough paper to get into the massive slaughter of Christians, so let me just comment on four events.

According to the old Testament, Moses was commanded by God to secure the release of his people from bondage. In his attempts to do so, thousands of innocent people, who had nothing to do with their King's decision to enslave Jews, died from the many plagues at Moses' hand. Just everyday Egyptians, people like you and I.

Next, Moses caused the death of each family's eldest son. How would you like your child murdered because George Bush would not obey the orders of a prophet, sent by God? In the end, Moses wound up destroying thousands of soldiers swallowed up by the Red Sea. Much like our troops in Iraq, they were just following orders from superiors.

It gets worse. When the slaughter had finally ceased, Moses gave his people God's Ten Commandments, one of which was "Thou Shall Not Kill."

I'M MOVING BACK TO MARS

And then there was Joan, a fifteen year old illiterate farm girl who, after many visions and hearing voices in her head since she was twelve, received a message from God to raise an army to kill the English. The fact that Saint Joan, just a child, was able to pull this off makes one want to believe it was God's will. Thousands were killed so Joan's form of Christianity could prevail in that tiny corner of the world. How many soldiers, at the brink of battle, knelt to pray that God would help them kill Englishmen. She died, burned at the stake, pleased with her crusades. Was God pleased with Joan for killing so many people?

Adolf Hitler, an atheist, wanted to rid God from the face of the planet. So in the name of that cause, he set out to take over the world. Killing Jews and ridding the world of Judaism was only a small part of his grand plan. Atheism would be the new religion and in the end, Hitler yearned for a superior Arian race who did not believe in God. His crusade almost succeeded and hung in the balance on the shores of Normandy for two days.

Finally, in the twenty first century, Osama bin Laden, known to be a great spiritual leader and prophet by thousands of his followers, has set out to rid the world of infidels and devils. (That would be you and me.) In the name of God and after much prayer, Osama blessed the death of thousands of innocent people at the World Trade Center and the Pentagon. "Praise be God," Osama prayed as the towers fell. He longs for a holy war with the evil ones, a war where God is on his side, where he can rally millions against us. While in hiding, he is winning in that effort. Look at the huge numbers of people on this planet who currently hate Americans. Make no mistake, Osama is considered the new prophet, sent by God, to kill all evil on this planet. In death, he will be honored as a great prophet and holy man by his followers.

And so we continue, progressing little, destroying human life in God's name. Man has always pondered his mission on this earth and I certainly don't have the answers. It seems we are doomed to stay here, repeating history, until we stop killing each other in the name of God.

In a thousand years will mankind still be killing his fellow man in God's name? If history is any barometer, the answer is yes.

He must be so disappointed in us.

SHE WAS NO "MOTHER TERESA" JUST A BLESSED EVENT

She was not even five feet tall and, with her shoulders slumped forward, she looked even shorter. We called her Mother Teresa because cops love to give nicknames to people who were unusual. Mother Teresa was most definitely unusual.

Each morning, just after dawn, she would dress in her dark cloak and place her prayer cloth over her head. Picking up her cane with a Jewish flag attached, she would leave her tiny efficiency and head for work. On most mornings, a cardboard box of Matzo-thins hung from a string around her arm. Even though she only lived a short distance from police

I'M MOVING BACK TO MARS

headquarters, it took her quite some time to get to work, shuffling along, but determined to complete her mission.

Mother Teresa's self appointed job was to bless things; everything, in fact. Starting in the police motor pool, she would pull a self made gizmo from her cloak with feathers on the end. Standing in front of each squad car, she would recite her blessings aloud in a language we later found was Polish, waving her blessing tool over each car. It would take her hours to work her way through the many cars in the pool. Then, she would slowly climb the front steps of the police station, stopping at each third step to rest. The large glass doors were too heavy for her to open so she would wait patiently for someone to exit and take advantage of the open door. Once inside, trouble would begin.

Mother Teresa took her work seriously. Blessing things was her profession. After working her way through the water fountains and complaint desk personnel, she would head for the restrooms. Entering the men's room, she would shock male visitors standing at the urinals by blessing them as they completed their mission.

Then, off to the Chief's office to give him her morning blessing. Finding the door locked, she would demand to enter. If the Chief was not busy, he would walk out to get his blessing, otherwise she would become indignant and pull a short, dead palm branch from her cloak, wave it in the air violently, placing a loud curse on everyone around her. Eventually, an officer would be called to escort her from the building. When he would gently grab her arm, she would resist as best she could, putting a double whammy curse on her assailant. In her excitement, she would loose control of her bladder, which really made a mess.

We only had her committed once. The psychiatrist's report concluded that, while she was a might eccentric, she was harmless. She loved God and felt her calling was to bless everything within her reach. Surely a large police department could tolerate a person who only blesses things, the report concluded.

For reasons I will never understand, I became the only person on planet Earth that could escort this woman from the building without a battle or a mess on the floor. The janitors loved me. It became a ritual. I would approach her smiling, extending my arm in a gentlemanly fashion and say, "Madam, may I have the honor?" After a quick blessing, she would slide her arm into mine and we would slowly leave the building.

Mother Teresa's visits lasted for about five years. Eventually she got too old to climb the front steps and had to settle for just blessing the motor pool and any officers who might be passing. She once got arrested in a supermarket for refusing to leave until she was finished blessing the cabbage. They, too, had the mops out.

I once drove by Mother Teresa, standing, slump shouldered, in a blinding, cold rain, clinging to a stop sign post and staring into space as her drenched cardboard Matzo box disintegrated. Like the rest of the world, I passed her by. Even though I am certain she would have refused my offer of a ride, I still regret, to this day, not stopping.

I'M MOVING BACK TO MARS

Abruptly, she stopped visiting us. Weeks later, her badly decomposed body was found on the floor of her flat. She had died of heart failure. We later learned she was not born Jewish, but a Catholic Pole, fleeing Poland with her parents just before Hitler took the country. (Many folks don't realize that Hitler also murdered Catholics.) Somewhere along the way, she adopted the Jewish faith. What happened after that was unclear. She had entered the U.S. through Ellis Island and was alone in the world. No family, no friends, just a crazy old coot, who had absolutely no one in her life.

I can't think of anything worse than being completely alone in the world. God was her only friend and that was fine with her. We buried her at pauper's field, next to One Arm Whitey, a derelict with a nasty disposition. She deserved better than to have to lie next to him. I miss Mother Teresa. Her picture still adorns my office wall and you know what? Her blessing would feel pretty good right now.

A WALK ON THE MOON

In The Cullasaja River Gorge

My wife and I owned a rappelling school in Highlands, North Carolina. This short story is based on one day of the 13 years we were in this thrilling business.

What do rappelling instructors do on their day off? They go rappelling.

Our packs full beyond their capacity, the three of us headed out into the cool, drizzly morning. The oversized ponchos draped over our bodies made us look like characters from a "Star Wars" movie as we trekked though the foggy, rain soaked forest, compass in hand, unable to identify the mountain ridge we needed to find our way. It seemed as if the fog would never lift.

Following our instincts, we reached the cliff's edge just as the rain stopped and the sun began to burn away the intense humidity. Soaked with perspiration, we dropped our packs and sat, staring at one another, gulping in air. After what seemed like an eternity of silence, Cindy spoke. "Dad, why are we doing this?" No one answered.

My friend, Dave, was the first to stand. He unzipped his pack and pulled the rope slings from their dry environment without a word. Why was everyone so quiet? Instinctively, we all got busy rigging the site for what was to become the most wild and crazy thing we had ever attempted. We would rappel the south wall of the Cullasaja River Gorge.

I had been staring at the cliffs since I arrived in Highlands in 1968. Big, bold and dangerous, they beckoned me. Every trip to Franklin, I would look at them across the vast gorge. Now, here I was, lifting 600 feet of rope on my back to begin the descent.

" See you at the bottom" is all I could think to say. This was not very original for a bold moment such as this. I started hacking my way through the ten feet of undergrowth near the cliff's edge and this proved to be more strenuous than I had anticipated. By the time I reached the granite face, my breathing was labored and my heart was pounding from excitement and fear.

Once I was in the clear, I turned to drink in the view. It was one of the most beautiful sights I had ever witnessed. Off my right shoulder, I saw the vast gorge widen before me toward Franklin. To my left, the threatening gorge deepened and narrowed. Turning in my harness I looked toward Highway 64 and saw another Dave, tiny as an ant, sitting on the guardrail, video camera poked in his eye. I took a deep breath and looked down between my legs. Far below, the tops of seventy foot pine trees seemed to point their limbs toward me. I could not see the bottom of my journey as it was just too far away.

I pulled rope from the oversized pack and slowly started my descent. A cool breeze blew across my face which seemed to calm me and give me confidence. It was remarkably quiet out on the face of the cliff. The only sounds were my feet crushing the sun dried lichen that had, long ago, attached itself to the sheer rock. I slowly descended, drinking it all in. There, in a small crack in the rock, green growth and a tiny white flower. Am I the first human to see this flower? Why am I so impressed?

Midway, I became overwhelmed with the vastness of this giant piece of granite rock. I felt so isolated, like a walk on the moon. Had any other human ever gone this way? There was so much barren, vertical rock. I felt so small, so insignificant. "Get a grip," I whispered softly and continued my descent.

When I reached the tops of the trees, I turned to wave goodbye to the camera man and lowered myself out of sight.

FRED WOOLDRIDGE

Seventy feet below, the terrain was hostile. I couldn't find a suitable landing spot. I moved horizontal across the face of the rock and suddenly, as if God were guiding me, I spotted a tiny, flat opening in the forest. I stopped just two feet from the forest floor, not wanting it to end. All alone, I stepped to the ground.

I am almost too embarrassed to tell you the antics I went through at the bottom. First there was dancing, then a couple of high fives against the granite, all the time talking and singing out loud. Then, in a moment of solitude, I leaned forward and kissed the rock. "I beat you, you @#$%&@."

Watching my daughter and Dave descend the wall was fun. There were hugs, high fives and hand shakes at the bottom. I never told them I kissed the rock, then cursed it.

Our trip out of the gorge was just as challenging and adventurous as our trip in but that's a story for another book..

THE KILLING MACHINE

A man's story

He was the perfect killer, professional, unemotional, methodical, disciplined and intelligent; a complete specimen, doing work for the grim reaper. Tall and thin, Bob was a rugged, handsome man with a full head of natural blond hair. His piercing blue eyes would always hide his true emotions. Killing people is what he did. After getting a good six hours of sleep, the stench of death still on his clothes, Bob would

I'M MOVING BACK TO MARS

awaken and kill some more.

It had taken just twelve weeks to transform Mrs. Fitzpatrick's little Bobby into a combat soldier for the United States Special Forces of the 82nd Airborne Division. Bob rounded out his training at sniper school.

He couldn't wait to get to Vietnam and quickly learned to hate the "Charlie." Bob took pride in knowing he had killed so many. After two years, he re-upped for another stint in the jungles and would eventually be the point man for the attack on the famed Hamburger Hill. Miraculously, he survived, receiving only minor wounds. Lying in a hospital bed, he felt his luck was running out and opted to leave the service, bringing home two Metals of Valor and several Purple Hearts, along with an array of other military commendations.

That is when I met Bob Fitzpatrick. He eventually became my point man on the Police Department's SWAT teams. Could Bob make the transition from the jungles to civilization? Time would tell.

He breezed through his police training and was top in his class for both academics and tactics. As class president, Bob was proud to have his wife, Debbie, pin his badge while holding his infant son, Cory.

He was the most disciplined SWAT officer I ever had the pleasure to work with. A person like him will do exactly what he is ordered, so the pressure is always on to make right decisions. Years later, with a drawer full of police commendations and awards, Bob came to me, asking for a transfer to the training unit. He was simply "burned out" from all the stress.

During a lunch break one afternoon, Bob said, "In Nam, you seldom got to look into the eyes of your enemy. With police work, it's more personal. Your enemy is right in your face and you get to stare into the eyes of the person who would kill you."

He adjusted well to his new job, setting up tactical training exercises for patrol officers. He had found his new niche.

Bob and I had a bond that goes far beyond just working together. There was a respect that only great fear can bring. During my first parachute "fun" jump, Bob was the guy who got me through it all and out that chopper door. On several special assignments, he watched my back, and once, saved my life.

During his tenth year as a policeman, Bob was carrying boxes of training manuals from his car to the office when he stepped on a crack in the sidewalk and turned his knee. He felt a sharp pain in his leg that wouldn't go away. Weeks later, after numerous trips to the doctor and lots of rehabilitation work, he finally gave in to his doctor's wishes to have surgery. It was a typical football injury. They would cut open his knee and sew everything back together. I agreed with his decision to have the surgery and reminded him of all the professional football players who have had this surgery and went on to play well in the NFL. I was glad about his decision as it was the only way he would be whole again. Bob would have been a lousy cripple.

Three days after surgery, Bob Fitzpatrick was dead. A large blood clot had dislodged from his knee and plugged his lungs and heart. It is so ironic that this man, who had faced so much danger in life, would step on a crack in the sidewalk and die. At his funeral, I choked twice during my prepared eulogy. I could not look into the eyes of his wife and son, sitting on the front row at church.

On quiet summer evenings, I sometimes sit on the deck of my mountain home, watching the moon set to the west. I think of Bob and all he had experienced. Volumes could be written about this man's adventures. I pray that God had mercy on this "killing machine."

FREDDIE, THE LEAF

With the fall season upon us, I thought it would be apropos to write about one of my favorite topics, the short children's story titled "Fall of Freddie, the Leaf" by Leo Buscaglia. Although the author deals directly with death in the kindest of terms, the story can take on many different meanings, especially for adults.

For those of you who may not be familiar with Freddie, let me tell you briefly he was a happy tree leaf who lived in a city park. He had many leaf friends and enjoyed his duties of providing shade for the people who visited the park to play and picnic. Freddie thought life would go on like this forever.

As fall came, Freddie, like all the other leaves in the park, began to change. He became afraid, so the wisest of all of Freddie's leaf friends told him not to worry, this was a natural thing, to turn color and eventually fall from the tree and die.

Freddie was stubborn and vowed never to die. As fall turned to winter, all of Freddie's friends turned brown and fell from the tree, leaving him behind. Freddie hung on, even though he was now lonely, shriveled and brown.

Finally he could last no longer and let go from his tree. As he fell away, Freddie could now see, for the first time, the entire tree where he had spent his life. It took on a new perspective and he could see his tree in relation to the other trees in the park. Freddie began to understand his role and purpose as a tree leaf. He knew that life would come back to the tree in the spring and that he would somehow be a part of that. As Freddie fell softly to the snow he was no longer afraid. He lay there peaceful with the knowledge that what was happening to him was a good thing.

Each fall season, I remember Freddie, the Leaf and then I remember an old, wise friend whose name was, like Freddie's author, Leo. He was a holy man, a police chaplain and the father of eight grown children. Leo was different, mostly because he never did or said what holy men were supposed to do or say.

He really did march to a different drummer and could always be found on the road less traveled. The police officers he counseled respected him. He survived, though, because no

I'M MOVING BACK TO MARS

one would dare question his deep and loving devotion to God. But Leo took a different approach to everything and I didn't realize it at the time but he and Freddie were friends. Leo was that wise old leaf who tried to counsel stubborn Freddie.

A long time ago, when I was a young man and thought that I knew everything about everything that anyone could know about anything, Leo sat down with me and tried to explain what an unwise man I was. He said "All of life's secrets, including the great mystery of death, lie right before your eyes. These are the things you should be focused on. You can't see because you are not looking. You are busy with other things and that is okay for now, but later, if you live long enough, take a good hard look at life and you will see it all."

Well, if Leo were still around today I would sit down with him and say, "I am beginning to get your point. For beginners, I am a 'Freddie the Leaf'. I like things just the way they are and want to put life on hold. Everything is changing though, including me, and I am resisting with all my might. I now have the time to do what you said, to look for those secrets of life that you said are right before my eyes. I am afraid to look, though, in fear that what I see I won't like. It is easier and much more comforting not to look. Thank you, but I'll just hang on to my tree."

So in the dead of this winter, when all the great trees are bare and snow covers the ground, if you see one single dead leaf still clinging to a tree, it is I.

FRED WOOLDRIDGE

INSURANCED OUT

My shorts are in a wad.

If I took every dollar I have ever given to insurance companies, I would have enough money to build a five story public restroom in Highlands, complete with gold plated accessories. I would certainly get more use from the restrooms than I have from my insurance policies. Forty cents of every dollar of my income is now given away for insurance of some kind and my shorts are in a wad.

I bought my first Florida home in 1959, a well built 1200 square foot, rectangular cookie cutter made of concrete. During the next 23 years, that little house withstood seven major hurricanes without damage, but my insurance company didn't care and the premiums went up and up and up each year.

Since 1958, I have never made an insurance claim for windstorm damage. Not ever. I attribute this to two things. I have always bought well built homes and I prepared well for hurricanes. The insurance companies have taken my 47 years of premiums, raked off their profit, and given the rest to those insurers who bought poorly constructed homes or did not prepare for hurricanes. Because there is not enough money to pay for damages, the companies raise everyone's rates each year. I know I shouldn't, but I resent paying for that.

Because of the heavy hit Florida took last year, insurance premiums are sky rocketing. Construction companies continue

I'M MOVING BACK TO MARS

to build homes that cannot withstand hurricane force winds and there are armies of home owners who just drive away and leave their homes to chance because the insurance will take care of it. A national insurance crisis is on the way, you can bet on it. Something's going to break, either the insured or the insurance companies.

Now that Highlands and nearby Franklin, North Carolina know the meaning and feel of a minimal hurricane, take a few minutes and ponder whether your mountain home would withstand 160 mph winds. I know mine wouldn't. Next time you're a passenger in a car on the interstate, stick your head out the window while moving 80 mph, keeping your mouth closed to prevent bugs on your teeth, and then double that. Got the picture? You can bet that insurance companies in these mountains are now reevaluating their assets and payouts for making premium increases. Insurance companies are not in the business of losing money.

Our national building codes place restrictions on the building of shabby homes. Permits are needed and code enforcement officers are quick to stop construction if standards are not kept or the proper materials are not used. That's fine.

Yet, not too far away from where you live, workers are gluing and stapling together cracker box homes with the cheapest materials possible that will blow apart in any sizable storm. Because they're on wheels and called trailer homes, (the key word being "trailer.") they don't fall under the purview of regular building codes. What an unfunny joke that is! Each year, a huge portion of everyone's insurance premium pays for the rebuilding or replacement of trailer homes, which the insurance companies and the trailer builders know will blow away in any sizable storm. They keep building and insuring them and storms keep blowing them away. Hello?

Then there is my car insurance premium which goes up each year while the value of my car goes down. Shouldn't the premium drop as the car decreases in value? God forbid I have an accident, even if I am not at fault, I'll be taken off the "safe driver" list and can expect a heavy increase the following year. What makes a person an unsafe driver when someone plowed into the back of them at a traffic light?

Then there is health insurance. For the price of health insurance each year, one could insure ten homes. Premiums are out of reach. Because God has blessed me with good health, I have practically never made a claim; I just pay and pay and pay. I know I shouldn't resent doing that, because I am healthy, but I do.

I will never collect on my life insurance policy because I've got to be dead to collect.

Finally, there is forced private mortgage insurance which protects the lender if an owner can't make mortgage payments. Shouldn't the lenders be buying that protection instead of us?

Excuse me but I am, plain and simple, just insured out.

I'M MOVING BACK TO MARS

ONCE UPON A TIME

Finding the mountains of Highlands.

Once upon a time there was a brilliant, powerful man by the name of Robert Thornhill. He lived in New York City and ran a conglomerate of small corporations, all generating great profit. Robert was the kind of man who loved working 16 hour days, needed little sleep and measured his success by the number of zeros on the end of his many bank accounts. Robert also had a knack of creating entrepreneurship in others and prided himself on the number of friends he had made into millionaires.

But as time went on, Robert became physically and mentally exhausted from his hard work. When he visited his doctor, he was told he was in poor health and should retire. The doctor knew Robert would never retire, but was able to convince him to take a vacation, something he had never done.

Surfing the Internet, Robert found Highlands and thought this just might be what he needed, a restful place, high in the mountains. So he jumped on one of his corporate jets and in a matter of hours, checked into one of Highlands' finest hotels.

On his third day in Highlands, Robert met a hillbilly named Billy Bob Cahill. Billy Bob was born in Highlands and loved his mountain life. He was a true mountain man, sporting bib overalls and a full beard. Thornhill spotted him walking to his truck one morning with a nice string of mountain trout. "Where did you catch those fish" Robert asked? "Can't tell 'ya, it's my secret place," Billy Bob responded. "Are you going to sell those trout? They're worth a lot of money." "Nah, don't much care about that. Got just enough here to feed my family, that's all I need."

The wheels inside Robert's head were spinning. "Mr. Cahill, I can make you a great deal of money. With me as your partner, I will set you up in a small corporation, selling your trout to my fish company in New York. Later, as business grows, we will open our own trout farm and generate even more business. In time you will own many, many trout farms and I will see to it that your corporation gets into the New York Stock Exchange. I can make you a millionaire in five years. Of course, you will have to move to New York and clean up a little. How about it?"

Billy Bob looked at Thornhill for a long time before responding. "Thanks a bunch for your offer but I am not interested. I catch just enough trout to feed my family, then I go home for lunch and take a nap. I whittle mountain hawks from solid blocks of oak for extra money. In the afternoon I play my banjo with friends and have trout for dinner. In the evening I make love to my wife and go to sleep. But thanks anyway."

Robert Thornhill was not a man you said no to, so each morning he would wait for Billy Bob at his truck and beg him to take the offer. Thornhill was a powerful salesman and, after much coaxing and pleading, convinced Billy Bob to catch some extra trout and sell it to Robert's New York fishery. In time Billy Bob began to enjoy the extra income and got caught up in the business, eventually gave up his mountain life to become a New York millionaire, working 16 hour days with little sleep. In time, he too became exhausted and went to his doctor.

The doctor looked Billy Bob square in the eye. "Ten years ago I told Robert Thornhill to retire and he didn't take my advice. Now he's dead. I'm giving you the same advice. Retire while you still have your health." As it turns out Billy Bob was wiser than Thornhill and he sold his corporation, all his fish hatcheries and his corporate stocks.

At his retirement party, a coworker asked Billy what he would do with his time now that he was a successful millionaire. Billy Bob leaned forward to speak into the microphone. "I'm going to a little place called Highlands. I'll catch trout for dinner and then take a nap. I will whittle mountain hawks from solid blocks of oak and play the banjo with my friends in the afternoon. After dinner, I will make love to my wife and go to sleep."

CELEBRATING THE PRINCE OF PEACE

Merry Christmas to all my readers.

Whether you are Jew, Muslim, Buddhist or Hindu, most non-Christian, peace loving, intelligent humans living today agree that Jesus Christ was special, a holy man of God, and a man of peace. Some non-believers go even further and call Jesus a great prophet.

Christians believe Jesus is all these things and more. We believe Jesus is the son of God; that he is God. We are about to celebrate His birthday, even though He was probably born in early fall, when censuses were usually taken. Most Christians agree this is their most important day of the year. We call it Christmas. Having given you all this information you already know, let me tell you something you may not know or even care about. Well, here I go anyway.

I was born a pagan. I didn't know of the Prince of Peace until I entered the first grade for the second time at the age of seven. I had flunked the first grade (can you believe it?) in public school, mostly for disorderly conduct and other anti-social behavior.

My parents, in a state of panic, sent me to a Catholic school, not for religious purposes, but because Catholic schools were big on discipline and torturing children. Later, I learned from my parents they had told the nuns, "Whatever it takes, you have our support." They didn't know you should never tell a school teaching nun, from that era, the sky is the limit. It took the school less than a year to straighten me out. Better still, they introduced me to Jesus Christ. For that and the discipline, I am eternally grateful.

Flash ahead sixty years since that first day at Saint Bridget's school and I will tell you my love for Jesus Christ has grown within me over the many years.

Furthermore, I am strongly aware of just how much my Christian religion is bound with Judaism. Although some Christians don't like to think about it, Jesus is a Jew. It is His heritage. The son of God is a Jew, making our two religions undeniably woven together. I believe that Christians and Jews should spend more time dwelling on that fact to better understand who we are and where we came from.

I'M MOVING BACK TO MARS

If you are a person who can only believe Jesus was just a man, then you must believe he was a good Jewish man who prayed in the Temples and celebrated the Passover. If you can just buy into that, then you must also believe He was a man of peace.

My belief is special, for I am convinced that Jesus Christ has saved me from dying many times. Up until I retired from the cliffs of Highlands, I have always had a risky job. That was my calling. I have had this sense that He was present, even in the worse times of my life, keeping me alive because He was not ready for me to leave life and move on. Hopefully He is not finished with me yet, even now, when the risks have waned. There seems to be a special bond I can't explain or prove. I just know it's there.

So on Christmas day, when Christian churches are filled to the brim to pay homage to the Son of God, our family will also gather together, pray and give thanks for all that we have been given. Afterwards, there will be presents, a meal with all the trimmings and lots and lots of laughter.

I will take time out from this busy, fun day, find a place where I can be alone, and again, privately thank Jesus Christ for allowing me to live this life.

No matter what religion you are, my wish to all of you is that you find love, kindness, and, most importantly, forgiveness in your heart on this day when Christians celebrate the birth of the Son of God, The Prince of Peace.

FRED WOOLDRIDGE

THE LIL MISSUS

Her friends still call her Saint Maddy!

She was only nineteen when I first laid eyes on her, a dark haired, brown eyed, French/Italian knockout. Maddy went to the beach with friends to work on her already perfect tan and swim in the ocean. I had done the same and now our blankets were less than twenty feet apart.

She went into the water and so did I. From her glances I was sure she was interested. At one point we were less than six feet apart but I was too timid to speak. Nothing happened.

After much coercing from my buddies, I decided to make my move. I strutted over to her blanket. "Anyone have a light?" (Is that corny?) In those days, everyone smoked but nerds. No one moved, except the lil missus, who offered her lighter. That was it.

I wonder, to this day, if she knew she would eventually become a policeman's wife, would she have been so quick with her offer. She has always said yes, but still I wonder. She was not happy the day I told her I had been accepted on the force but she never interfered or objected.

Maddy worked for the FBI in Miami for ten years before our first child was born. Now, with a son in our home, the announcement of another policeman's death took on a deeper concern for her. Then there was a second child, then another. How would she ever raise three small children if her husband was killed? Miami became more dangerous with each passing day.

Life got even harder for her the day I was assigned to work narcotics. Little did either of us know I would spend the next ten years working dope, four of those undercover. It was a scary time for both of us.

At church on Sunday, Maddy would march down the aisle with her three small children and her dirt bag husband in tow. I had hair to my shoulders and a scruffy beard. People would shake their heads in disbelief at how such an attractive woman with those lovely children could get hooked up with such a slimy character. But the lil missus never allowed herself to be embarrassed. She held her head high with the personal knowledge that her husband was taking drug dealers off the street. She could tell no one.

When the phone rang at three in the morning, she would wake with a jolt and pray it was not the call all police officers' wives dread. It happened often. This time, I had gone to work in the afternoon and was now calling to tell her I was in New York on a drug buy. I would not be home for days. You just can't imagine what she went through unless you personally experienced it.

She went to a few funerals with me. One, an FBI agent and good friend, Ben Grogan, had been gunned down in the street during a wild shootout in Miami. The sorrow was overwhelming and she couldn't help but think if her time to grieve for me was coming soon. It never did. I eventually retired and life became a little calmer for both of us.

Adding to her stress, there was rappelling. Our youngest son was only six when I first coached him off a hundred foot cliff, much to Maddy's disbelief. She sat quietly for years as I taught each child how to play on the cliffs. The torture of watching them step out on the precipice was unnerving for her. She never interfered, knowing I would do nothing that would harm them. Eventually, she put on the harness and stepped from that same 100 foot cliff. She was, and still is, such a good wife and mother.

When I write, she is my first and most crucial critic. An "A" student in English and grammar, almost nothing gets by her. Sometimes she applies tough love. We debate, she wins, and I continue writing. How can she be smarter than "spell check?"

We have been married forever. (Don't ask!) Through all the good times and some really bad times, there was always love, sometimes strong, sometimes seemingly nonexistent, but it was, and is, always there.

When it is time for Maddy to meet with her maker, she will simply say to the Lord, "I was married to Fred Wooldridge" and POW, the gates will open.

THE END

Made in the USA
Coppell, TX
10 December 2022